Mark,
So grea~
Perhaps will don~
the A + C puking lot again...
XO · Tq~

WALKING THROUGH

SHADOWS

WALKING THROUGH
SHADOWS

TARA
MANUEL

thistledown press

Thistledown Press Ltd.
118 - 20th Street West
Saskatoon, Saskatchewan, S7M 0W6
www.thistledownpress.com

Library and Archives Canada Cataloguing in Publication

Manuel, Tara, 1973-
Walking through shadows : stories from the edge of the world / Tara Manuel.
Short stories.
ISBN 978-1-897235-86-7

I. Title.
PS8576.A575W35 2011   C813'.6   C2011-901711-3

Cover photograph by Özgür Donmaz (istockphoto.com)
Author photo by Mike Spenser
Cover and book design by Jackie Forrie
Printed and bound in Canada

Canada Council   Conseil des Arts   Canadian   Patrimoine
for the Arts   du Canada   ARTS BOARD   Heritage   canadien

Thistledown Press gratefully acknowledges the financial assistance of the Canada Council for the Arts, the Saskatchewan Arts Board, and the Government of Canada through the Canada Book Fund for its publishing program.

WALKING THROUGH
SHADOWS

For Michael

CONTENTS

Take my arm, I'll do you no harm. I only smoke cigars — *Simon Manuel*

THE BUTTERFLY

WHEN HER LOVER ENTERS HER SHE LETS her secret sounds come out. They crescendo, spike, and ebb, like wings negotiating a squall. He is the only one she makes her sounds for, he with his gnarled brown hands, fingernails thick with age, he is the one who gives her the hot feeling inside that makes her fly. When the encounter is over, she pulls her jeans back on and accepts his offer of rainwater tea. She watches him as he collects water from the cut off pop bottles he keeps outside the van, and boils it in his electric kettle. They sit sipping together, she tall and thin like a crowded black spruce reaching for the light, and he, the bearded "Arab", small and sinewy from a life of hard living. They watch the world through the dirty Plexiglas window in his camper van at the side of a ravine off the old railway bed. He's lived here a long time in the van without wheels that, as time goes on, threatens to be reclaimed by the land. Moss covers much of the lower third of his home, here and there its green surface broken with holes the cats have made. There are many cats, half feral, too many to count. Cats that repay his kindness of regular feeding with their warmth on bitter winter nights.

The girl puts her stained cup down on the desiccated Formica mini-table and stands up. She touches his face, skin like old, brown leather, and slips her fingers back into his hair, an uncultivated grey bundle he tucks under his hat whenever he goes out. He reaches for her hand and kisses it gently, his smiling mouth remembering the time long ago when it had all its teeth.

"You're goin' now are you? Well, you go on my dear, but get back into town to your mother now before it gets dark."

She towers over him, curling her back to stand in the cramped space. Her tongue silent again, she pats his head and turns, pushing open the door and stepping out into the sky. She flits along the old railway bed, but not in the direction of town. There's a little while yet before night comes, and she flutters this way into the interior, along the trail left behind when the old train tracks were removed. The trail winds deep into barren, desolate places, through thick boreal forests, and out along wind-swept coasts. She reaches her hand out, plucks an alder leaf, and holds it under her nose. The perfume smells old and new at the same time.

The girl is looking for something lost. She doesn't know what it is, it's not a conscious thought, rather an eternal yawning need expressed through erratic wandering. Her movements are quick and light, her body slim and lithe. She has a handsome face, with strong, almost masculine features that lend a certain gravity to her demeanor. Her hair, cut short by her mother, is dark brown and whip straight.

After a time of seeking without finding, after peering through thick underbrush, and further on, scanning endless bog on either side of the trail, she turns toward town, her feet barely touching the dusty old railway bed. Often when she walks her sounds will come, only if she is alone though, it wouldn't do for anyone else to discover her ability, so much has come to depend upon her state of silence.

The house she lives in is on the opposite side of town from her lover's grounds, and rather than travel in straight lines, the girl meanders up and down residential streets. She passes like a shadow, flickering past lives without leaving a trace of herself. While within the town she tries to lock her sounds inside, but sometimes they escape, trick her, make themselves without her hearing, and then perhaps a person sitting in the dark on their front stoop might wonder if they heard the mute girl speak.

When she arrives at the door of the little three-roomed hovel where her mother waits, she gives her fingers a blow and tries for a silent turn of the knob. She holds her breath and stoops as she passes the threshold. Her mother, sitting in her dusty-rose armchair in front of the rabbit-eared TV, swivels around, her dyed blonde chin-length hair a solid unmoving crust upon her head.

"You're home now, are you my dear? Fill me teacup up for me, will ye? I can't get up now my toe is that bad." Not expecting a response, she swivels back toward the TV.

"I got to try to get in to see Doctor tomorrow now, please God, if they'll take me, it's killing me to walk."

The girl brings the teacup filled with hot kettle water and lays herself down to nest for the night on the long couch which her mother has spread with, first the flannel sheet, and then the scratchy wool blanket. On the top she has placed the fleece blanket with the pussycat on it, which will pass the night being worried between the long fingers of the girl's hand.

She turns onto her side, watching the coloured lights from the screen play off her mother's face. The deep colours of her makeup are never more at home than in a dark room in front of the screen. This is where her mother belongs, not in the sunlight where the red cheek circles, the fuchsia-smeared lips, and the blue-black rimmed eyes dripping with mascara are so wrong the birds flee in terror.

The girl gets up to stoke the wood stove before turning herself to the inside, away from the glare, closing her eyes and going deep inside. Way down inside her there is a dream that has come so often its closeness is like family. It's always the same: the long dark hair of a man taller than the sky rising and falling behind him as he lopes away from her, his legs so long that the pace he sets is impossible for her to sustain as she pines to catch up with him, grasp his brown hand and make him turn to reveal his face. She knows this dream has something to do with the stories the people have told in her presence, forgetting that silence and stupidity are not the same thing.

She has heard the good people whisper about the brown stranger who came to town many years ago when the trains still rumbled through, bringing with them a glimpse of the world beyond. He hated to travel in the modern way, they said, and couldn't bear but to use his own two legs to transport him through the world. So he got off. She has heard them talk, too, about her mother and her fetching looks as a young girl, fetching in the way an average girl of a certain age will stand out in a small out-of-the-way place. They said her mother and the long-haired stranger went walking together, said it in a knowing way, and that before he disappeared, he was seen walking out of town on the canal road toward the great lake in the interior wearing a woman's purple ski jacket and carrying nothing but a fly rod.

"Micmac," they called him, and it sounded like spitting.

She wakes at the first hint of dawn, with the first song of the white-throated sparrow performed from the spruce trees surrounding their house. She springs up, opens the wood stove door and pokes at the last struggling embers for a moment before giving up and starting the fire from scratch. She crumples up newspaper to start the flame, newspaper she has not bothered to read, and sits on her slender haunches to wait patiently for the kindling to catch. She reads stories in the flames, stories that are half formed in her mind. They have to do with the beginning of the world, not in the way the beginning is preached from the pulpit of the big church where the people, decked out in fancy clothes, speak in silly tongues, but the beginning as she remembers it. A time when the world was dark, and the creatures had no light with which to see. Many tried and failed to bring back flame from the sun and the world remained in darkness until mother spider silently, without the knowledge of the others, spun a long thread and travelled to the sun carrying with her a clay pot. She took the flame from the sun and placed it inside the pot so quickly that she was not burned. Then she brought it home to the others, gave it to them and, without a word, slipped away to live in silence. From then on the world enjoyed light, but not one of the creatures remembered how they had received it in the first place.

The girl does not ask herself how she knows her stories, but just lets them come and tell themselves to her. Then her sounds come, and she is unaware of them making themselves as she rocks back and forth in front of the flame. When the fire is right she closes the door and fills the kettle to put on the cooking stove. She makes herself some tea and has bread with peanut butter and, before her mother wakes, she brushes her teeth and is off out the door, stooping for a split second to grasp some spearmint leaves growing out of the ditch in front of the house. She takes them in her mouth and chews, enjoying the clean flavour.

There are chores she must perform to ensure that life continues evenly for her and her mother. One of these is the twice-weekly trip to the local food bank. It is run by one of the many church groups out of the basement of a member's house in a narrow cement-floored room lined with plywood shelves. The girl will wait patiently as one of the good ladies fills her bags for her, making the wisest choices on behalf of her silent customer. In the natural way of most speaking people when confronted with a still tongue, they shout at her kindly, as if she were deaf or hard of understanding. The girl does not take offense. It's a small price to pay, really, for the privilege of eating. As she turns to go, her strong arms laden with bags, she hears the plump lady who served her whisper to the rotund new woman at the back, continuing a conversation her need had interrupted,

"He's been seen a few times since over the years, you know, and she's the spit of him. The very spit." And then she calls out cheerily, "Bye now, my dear, say hello to your mother for me!"

The girl returns to her house, drops the bags on the counter for her mother to sort through and is off once again. She crosses the old railway bed and makes her way onto Main Street, a desolate place where many of the storefronts have been boarded up, yet the lights which line it still shine at night, ever hopeful that life will return. In the distance she spies her lover's bicycle, a sorry heap of corroded metal, propped up against the brick ledge outside the bar. He's at it early this morning, a sure sign it's that time of the month; the welfare checks are in. When she reaches the bicycle, she leans forward, pressing her face to the mirrored window. She spies him at his customary perch in front of a VLT, a glass of beer on the table at his side, and she knows he won't leave until he's well drunk and has surrendered all his money to the machine with the lights. He's too engrossed in the machine to take notice of her, and she watches him for a second, his round tan hat on his head, the one he always wears, the one that looks like a turban from a distance, his collared shirt thin with wear, an old brown woolen jacket at his side. She leaves him there — that's how it is. Their love is a secret pleasure, a room without windows in this town full of helpful, ever-watching eyes.

She turns and begins walking in the way of the water, downhill toward the lake. She skips, she hops, she moves lightly through the little world of the town, down to the streets near the beach, all built up now with massive fancy houses owned by respectably fat ladies and their very busy men.

She skirts the red, sandy shore all the way to the other side of the lake and continues further to where it bends and dips, and bends again to create a private place where a girl may bathe in peace. She stands shock still, listening into the distance for the sound of an ATV. Hearing none, she slips off her sneakers, socks, and jeans, her panties and pink V-neck top. In this little cove, the shallow water at the sandy edge gives way quickly to deep black, and this makes it perfect. The girl immerses herself swiftly, using her hands to wash her private places, scrub her hair against her scalp, and caress her belly that will never swell with child. She rubs herself vigorously, so that even her insides with their tubes tied for her own good will come clean.

Afterwards, she stands for a moment, letting her skin dry in the sun and the sharp wind. She closes her eyes and raises up her arms, fingers separate and reaching. The distant hum of an engine gives her cause to hurry and she dresses quick as a flash and commences her search once again.

She awaits the fall of night before treading the path to her lover's place. When the last of the playboys on their dirt bikes have roared toward the lights of town, when the trouting men have mounted their ATVs and driven home, then she makes her way to the little van in the trees by the ravine. The van is silent tonight, his bicycle with its basket laden with groceries abandoned on the ground outside, and when she steps through the open door and into the cramped space, the cats are the only ones to greet her. They twist and writhe about her ankles; they mew up at her as if willing her to speak.

Her lover lies passed out on his stained pull-down cot, his hat falling off his head, thinly soled shoes still on his feet. He emits a powerful stench of stale beer and tobacco, but underneath she catches his true scent, the scent of the woods, of coniferous sap, of perfumed alder catkins, of dry red soil. The girl is not repulsed by him, this man of meager means. She feels no matronly pity for him either. He is the one who helps her fly; this is his earthly disguise. But there will be no flying tonight. She carefully unties the many knots in her lover's shoelaces, and places his shoes on the floor at the side of the bed. His body lies twisted, like a piece of driftwood. She covers him with a grey army blanket, sits on the little bench, and turns to the window. From this place she can just spy the trail through a break in the alder thicket and, as she keeps watch, her sounds come.

Her sounds are ancient, guttural, wordless songs. She lets them come now, without fear of her lover waking, and the sounds rise and rise in intensity until they make their waves, sound waves she imagines she can see emanating from her and moving outward in perfect circles to envelop the trees and the earth and the sky and all the creatures living between them. And the sound circles grow larger and larger. They encompass the forest with its deep, scarred places and continue until they reach the great lake and it, too, is embraced within her circle of sound. This is as large a circle as she can create, and as the girl sits staring wide-eyed through the dirty glass into the break in the trees beyond, holding her last note for as long as her breath will sustain, she sees something flash before her eyes. In that second through the split in the trees she sees a thing streak by. She leaps up from her seat at the window and dives through the open door, landing on the mossy ground with barely a thud so quick is she to roll onto her lightning feet. She jumps through the tangle of cats and on toward the path through the trees.

The girl emerges from the trail onto the old railway bed, and turns instinctively toward the forest. She glimpses a whipping mane of brown hair streaked through with grey turning the corner ahead of her, and she runs faster, more skillfully than she has ever done, her body knowing this is the test it was preparing for all those silent years. As she rounds the bend in the near darkness, she spies the thing in the distance. Taller than all other men, he moves away from her on swift feet. She races after him, and, just as in her dream, she feels a profound longing to reach out her hand and have it enclosed in his. She pursues her quarry along the dusty path into the night, her nose tipping skyward, hoping to catch his scent. She runs and runs, but the faster she runs, the larger grows the distance between them. With a final burst, she stretches out her long arms, her slender fingers trying to catch hold of him. But he is gone. In the space the road has made there extends only blackness for as far as the girl can see. She stands still for a moment, before turning and walking silently along the dark path back toward town, where far away in the little house her painted mother sits in the glare of the coloured lights awaiting her return.

THE WHITE PRINCE

HE SLIDES OUT OF HIS TOP-OF-THE-LINE silver SUV, one perfectly polished brogue caressing the only sidewalk in town. This is his town, the one his family has ruled for two generations, and he is the glad result of their careful breeding, not an insignificant challenge in this isolated place. He is, he believes, in his middle-aged splendour, the finest thing on offer to God and man. He secretly refers to himself as The White Prince.

Bruce Hancock, referred to deferentially as "Minister" by most of the town's good citizens, arrives at his office exactly on time. The building, out of which he works as representative in the provincial legislature for the people of his district, is the only brick building in town. It alone among the town's other structures of wood and vinyl bears the dignity of stone, and it carries its stature with great modesty. It is perfectly fitting then, that this attractive two-story edifice should count among its inhabitants the most illustrious member this district has ever had the honour of voting for.

The White Prince enters the foyer of his office with an upbeat and pleasant "Good Morning!" issuing forth from his perfectly formed mouth. His smile reveals agreeably shaped sparkling white teeth, which draw attention away from his wattle, the unfortunate side effect of too many motel meetings and fundraiser luncheons. Still, his looks are impressive, he thinks, as he beams down from a great height at his plump and shining assistant. He is aware that she feels, as do all women when he smiles upon them, as if for that moment she is the only woman in the world his brilliant pale-blue eyes find worthy of contemplation. And when she speaks, he listens with such rapt interest to her words that his practiced intimacy makes her believe they must be the most interesting, the most elucidating his small tidily shaped ears have ever had the pleasure of hearing.

"Bruce, the mayor is hoping to meet with you this morning to discuss the provincial government's contribution to the municipal road work," she says, imagining her words have a deeper, more subtly flirtatious connotation, and she blushes as he leans in, speaking to her in his confidential way.

"Well, my lovely Brenda, why don't you invite him to meet me at the motel for a long working lunch and we'll do our best to sort things out?" He smiles down at her, his eyes with their winking, saucy, irresistible charm doing to her what they do to any person who finds themselves in the envious position of being in close proximity with this man-god.

"Right away, Minister," she breathes, picking up the phone to make the call as The White Prince enters his office and softly closes the door.

Bruce takes his place at his large oak desk, and begins, as he always does, with his correspondence. There are letters from constituents outlining, with various degrees of literacy, their particular problems and requesting his help in finding solutions. Bruce does best in this area of his work. A phone call here, a letter to the right person there, and a problem can be very quickly solved. Perhaps a municipal decision over-turned, a child hired for summer work, or a piece of crown land leased at a bargain, and the recipient of the help can be counted upon to continue voting in his favour. This kind of hands-on approach is the secret to his success. What do the larger issues matter when each person feels his or her own small need is his greatest concern?

Everyone will agree that his success in fifteen years as elected member has been enormous; however, the amazing thing is that, if pressed, most people would have trouble pinpointing the exact nature of his accomplishments.

On this morning Bruce is having trouble keeping his mind on his work. Someone has captured his attention, and against his better judgment, his mind has been playing at ways of orchestrating an intimate meeting. He drops his beautiful head of whitening hair into his hands, and squeezes, as if trying to wring out the last drop of desire.

Since that nasty business with his wife, a tragedy felt by all, he's gone out of the way to keep private his little pleasures. They lived separate lives inside their home, still, he does not wish her memory to be sullied by talk of his proclivities. Not to mention the reaction from the Church of the Everlasting Evangelical, his church, where he enjoys the status of most cherished member. No, he must appear above reproach; it's so important for the common people to have someone to look up to, someone who will not disappoint them by being human. And if he has to fake the speaking in tongues to set a good example, well what's the harm in that? It's not difficult once one takes the mind out of the equation, and, after all, his ability acts as a catalyst for others to find their own forgotten languages. He's doing them a favour, is he not? It just wouldn't do for him to admit he's never really been taken by the spirit, and his agility with ancient tongues is all an act of charity.

The White Prince, unable to restrain himself any longer, stands up, pinches his keys, and deserts his desk, telling himself that sometimes a man just has to please himself first.

"I forgot I was supposed to see someone at the airport for a quick meeting." He offers this to Brenda as an explanation for his hasty departure.

Bruce cruises his spotless ride around the staff parking section of the airport lot, searching for the old Ford pickup truck, which, he remembers, will most certainly be covered with mud. Spotting it in the far corner, a scratched wooden kayak secured on the roof rack, he feels his heart leap, and his scalp begin to tingle.

"Easy does it, control, control," he says to himself, quickly regaining his composure. He takes for himself a VIP parking spot, knowing with measured certainty that he will not be ticketed.

The White Prince, impressive in his linen suit, does not enter the terminal, rather, he walks around to the fenced tarmac, waves to one of the security workers who comes to greet him and unlock the gate. The good minister is known for his impromptu visits, and under the pretence of gaining a firsthand understanding of the new security implementations on the tarmac side of the airport operations, he makes his way swiftly toward the other workers. He chats with each of them, feigning complete absorption in their descriptions of the new measures, all the while his eyes straying briefly to scan the area for the object of his desire.

When his eyes fall upon the person they seek, Bruce turns quickly back to the man he's been chatting with, forces himself to maintain his casual demeanor, fighting down the rush of excitement. He smiles, nodding his head, having no idea any longer what the man is saying. As soon as a pause occurs,

Bruce excuses himself and, as casually as he can manage, strides on his long legs toward the luggage trolley.

Sensing his approach, the young man turns, his honey-blond, curly hair shining in the sunlight, his muscles bulging as he lifts a large duffle bag out of the chute and places it on the trolley. He smiles at Bruce, Derek's head nodding sharply back in greeting.

The White Prince sucks in his little potbelly and stops, smiling in his inviting way, holding out his hand. As Derek removes his work glove to accept the gesture, there passes between them a powerful vibration and Bruce must fight with himself to control his growing agitation.

"This job keeps you in great shape I see."

"Yeah, not too bad." The young blue-eyed man, obviously pleased with the compliment, smiles and waits for the minister to continue. Overwhelmed for a moment by the almost feline beauty of the creature before him, The White Prince invents an excuse for his approach.

"I noticed you have a kayak on the top of your truck. Do you go out much?"

"Almost every evening when the weather's fine."

"I was thinking of buying a kayak myself, trying to get back in shape, you know, but there's nobody locally who gives lessons." Bruce waits to see if he'll bite.

"Aw," says the blond beauty, swiping dismissively at the air between them, "I could take you out and show you a few things; you'd take to it in no time."

"Yeah?"

The White Prince calculates how much time he'd need to get into the city, purchase a kayak and paddle, and get his work done. Then, censuring himself for his eagerness, he suggests, "What about tomorrow night?"

"Sure," says the young man, surprised at the minister's definite plans, "I'm off tomorrow so — any time you want, I guess."

What Bruce really wants to suggest is dinner at his house, but not wanting to arouse suspicion, he says casually, "I should be finished everything about six-thirty. How would that be — Derek isn't it?"

Derek, obviously pleased that the minister would know his name, smiles widely and nods his head.

"Where do you usually go?" asks Bruce, his mind reeling with possible scenarios.

"Aw, different places, out on the coast if I have a lot of time, but there's lots of places close to town where I paddle too."

"Any place where we won't run into anglers or boats?" inquires Bruce. He wants to tie up their plans quickly and depart lest his attention to the young Derek arouse the enmity of one of his many fans.

"Oh yeah, we could put in at the bridge and go up into Lot's Brook, you know, the one that was cut off when they put the dam in. There's old Indian ground up there," he speaks, his face flushed. "I found a couple of arrowheads there awhile back."

"You don't say. That sounds great, Derek. Shall we meet at the bridge then, six thirty?"

"Sure, all right."

"So — see you then." Bruce smiles and turns, resisting the urge to touch his hand again. I didn't get to where I am today by giving into every base urge, he thinks, congratulating himself for showing such restraint. The White Prince returns to his vehicle the same way he came, and drives back to his office in the centre of town feeling like the cat that ate the canary. He will have to proceed most carefully now; this sort of business would be poison to his career. He has always taken the greatest pains to indulge his needs elsewhere, on trips to faraway places where society looks more kindly upon the particular requirements of fine western middle-aged men. To sully his patch at home would be near fatal. Why then, is he acting in such a reckless a manner? Bruce pushes the question back — his instincts have always served him well.

When he returns to the office, his eyes bright with excitement, Brenda is waiting.

"Bruce, the members of the committee are waiting in the boardroom — the meeting was supposed to start ten minutes ago," she chides gently, handing him a folder and helping him off with his jacket. Bruce, a leading member on many committees, struggles to remember which group he is to meet with this morning. What does it matter? he says to himself — they're all the same anyway. The usual round of do-gooders with a smattering of different members here and there for good measure. He enters the florescent-lit room with gusto, bids everyone a "Good Morning!" and in his charmingly self-effacing manner, apologizes for his tardiness.

Still unaware of which meeting he has joined, Bruce comfortably assumes his role of chair. "Great! Let's get started. Which of you would like to bring me up to date on the progress we've made since our last meeting?"

His request is eagerly met by a sturdy committee lady, a retired teacher in her sixties who, Bruce remembers, sits on several other committees as well. As she speaks, the tedium of her voice cracking with the effort of enunciating every word clearly lulls Bruce into a reverie. He is on the water behind Derek; their strokes bring an even rhythm to their movement across the black water of the river. Bruce watches the ripple of muscle under the thin cotton of the young man's shirt as he paddles, his long elegant fingers gripping the shaft and Bruce, seeing those hands against his own skin, dares to hope they might give him what he so darkly desires.

He snaps to attention then, realizing that everyone is waiting expectantly for him to speak. "Thank you, Madeline, for that update," he smiles. "Does anyone have any suggestions for how we should proceed from this point?" he asks, not allowing the fact that he has no idea what this meeting is about to impede the progress and inevitable success of the project.

"I suggest we decide on a date for the fundraising concert, pick a church to 'old it in, and discuss who we should ask to perform," suggests the committee lady, a model of logical, if not vocal, efficiency. Now Bruce remembers which particular group this is and, as the committee members bicker over which church would best deserve this particular function, he gathers his papers and stands up.

"I'll leave it to you capable people to make the arrangements we discussed. Someone will have to put a package together to give to the various media, but as I will of course be emceeing the event, it will have to be someone other than myself. Good work today, folks!" The White Prince makes his exit and the room is silent for a moment in his wake as the various committee members marvel at the minister's tireless ability to pull a project together.

The following day seems to go on without end as Bruce anticipates, with relish, his meeting with Derek. When five o'clock finally comes, The White Prince enters the front door of his large ranch-style home with its two-car garage. It sits splendidly facing the road, its enormous windows beautifully but heavily curtained, its sizeable backyard tastefully but completely enclosed. He locks the door. This is his sanctuary.

He'd had it completely done over the year after his wife died. She'd loved bright colours and the house had begun to resemble a technicoloured dream coat. Bruce, after his own fashion, had everything done in white. He'd ordered in a white leather sofa set for the living room, white rugs, blinds, and double-lined curtains. He'd had the kitchen redone in gleaming stainless steel and white marble, and it looked as if it had never been used. The main bathroom, he'd left as it was, in respectful memory of his wife. It had been the only room in the house she'd hadn't had the opportunity of imposing her exuberant love of colour on and it remained white, the gleaming jet powered bathtub set on a ceramic tiled pedestal remaining as a testimonial to her tragic fate. Bruce could not enter this room without seeing his wife as he'd discovered her seven years before, sprawled face-down naked on the tile, a vivid pool of blood surrounding her head. Died instantly, they told him, slipped and hit her head. He wished he could get that image out of his mind. It made it difficult for him to truly enjoy the fruits of his labours. Perhaps, thinks The White Prince, it is time to have the bathroom redone. Time to forget.

Bruce, checking the time, decides he has enough to have a soak before the scheduled delivery of his new kayak. He pours himself a generous glass of sparkling white wine and carries it into his expansive bedroom to undress as the bath pours. He stands admiring his figure in the full-length mirror. Yes, I have let myself go a little, he chastises his reflection. He turns and runs an appraising hand up the back of his leg and over his right buttock. He watches himself, lifting his hand away and smacking his bottom forcefully, the sound ricocheting off the walls. He bends over, and smacks again, this time harder, causing the wine to splash onto the rug.

It's just not the same when he does it himself. He stands up then and grabs a towel to dab the wet spot on the carpet. He gets into the tub, turns on the jets, and lies back, picturing the figure of the young Derek. He cautions himself to proceed most carefully, his body humming with the prospective rewards of a good hunt.

Bruce has the delivery guy help him secure the brand new kayak on the roof rack of his SUV. It's the first time he's used the rack for its intended purpose, and as he sets out toward the bridge he feels like a much younger man on the precipice of an adventure. Derek is sitting in his truck smoking a cigarette, and when Bruce pulls up he flicks it out the window and hops out to greet him.

"Nice boat."

"Let's see how nice, shall we?"

"Sure thing." Derek releases the strapping on his own boat and deftly lifts it off the truck and places it neatly onto the riverbank. He glances at Bruce, and sensing his need, goes to his aid and takes over. Bruce watches in admiration.

They set off, paddling upriver, the reedy banks on the far side thrumming with damselflies. The two men cross over the river toward the reeds, damselflies fluttering all around, their bodies brilliant green, bronze wings tipped with black. Bruce smiles and looks ahead to admire Derek's hands as they handle the paddle. It's just as he'd imagined. They continue upstream awhile and where the river begins to widen, Derek leads them back across, parrying against the current. The wind picks up and Derek shouts back to Bruce, pointing in the direction of a large tributary.

"That's where I found the arrowhead!"

"Show me!"

They turn into the tributary and paddle far enough that the river disappears behind them around a bend in the shore. Here, out of the wind and the current, the air is still for a time, until the slap of a large beaver tail between the boats breaks the stillness. Derek turns around, catching Bruce's eye. He smiles and motions toward a small clearing atop the far bank. They paddle toward the shore, Derek getting out first and pulling Bruce's boat onto the sandy beach so he won't have to get his feet wet. Derek hangs his spray skirt on a tree branch and reaches toward Bruce to take his.

The young man efficiently gathers wood and starts a fire. With his knife, he cuts a slim branch off a fallen tree, makes a "y" shape, and digs the long end into the sand beside the fire. He takes from his pack an old tin can with wire strung through the sides, and scoops up river water. He hangs the kettle from the branch, fussing with it until he has it positioned well over the flame. Bruce watches his every capable movement.

"Cup of Tetley?" Derek asks, smiling a little shyly now at Bruce.

"Sure. You're well prepared."

"Always."

They drink their tea in silence, looking out over the water to the evergreen forest on the far shore. The silence between them grows, fraught with a tension Bruce is no longer able to hide. He drinks the last of his tea and puts down his cup in the pebbly sand. He turns over onto his belly, alongside the lovely Derek. With a tentative movement that surprises Bruce, Derek puts his cup down and assumes the same position, belly down on the beach. The evening sun caresses their backs, the water is calm and silent. The White Prince does something then that he will always think of later in his life as being one of the riskiest, most foolhardy actions he has ever committed.

He raises his long elegant hand up into the air, his fingernails clean and buffed, their smooth surface glinting in the evening sun, and brings it down as hard as he can onto Derek's backside, the sound smacking off the bank. Derek reels around, staring wide-eyed at Bruce, his mouth open in shock. And then he takes action. He opens his hand and slaps the minister across the face so hard Bruce falls back, covering his face in his hands. The young man kneels up and with one ferocious pull, yanks down Bruce's athletic shorts and proceeds to whale on his bottom, smacking with the flat of his hand, a forceful rhythmic beating. Bruce can hardly believe his luck.

He accepts the beating with relish for a short time, then twists around and grabs Derek, wrestling him to the ground beside him, and growls into his ear, "Why don't we finish this at my place after dark — you come on foot."

"All right, Minister," Derek whispers, out of breath now with the effort of the struggle. Bruce releases him then, and Derek goes about the business of putting out the fire and collecting teacups without a look in Bruce's direction. They set out, wordlessly, back down the river. When they reach the bank by the bridge, Derek gets out first and pulls Bruce's boat onto the shore, holding it steady while he steps out. He flips the minister's boat over easily onto his shoulders and carries it to the silver SUV. He secures it to the roof rack while Bruce stands watching, a Mona Lisa smile gracing his handsome middle-aged face.

The White Prince enters his sanctuary. He goes from room to room closing blinds, fussing with the placement of the double-lined curtains. He goes out into the garage and opens the door a crack. Not enough to notice from the street, but enough space for a strong young hand to slide in and open. He returns to the house and sits, surveying his dominion, waiting for night to fall.

THE WALKING LADY

BABS GOES WALKING. EVERY NIGHT AFTER THE dishes are done, after the debris of day is swept from the kitchen floor, she layers up, calls "I'm gone now, love", over her shoulder to Wince, and sets out. Wince, cocooned in his ratty leather armchair by the wood stove, smiles down at his knitting.

She walks this hill, lined with modest houses, up to the trail that leads to the canal. Everyone on the street knows her by now, they know her habits too, and nod in admiration without attempting to draw her into conversation. They know she's not out for a social. She's the walking lady. And at fifty-five years, she's in better shape than most local women half her age.

At top walking speed, Babs can reach the banks of the canal in fourteen minutes. No panting, no searching for breath. Her powerful legs pump smoothly and efficiently; hard arms slice the air, propelling her forward. This is her favourite part of it — the long dirt road by the canal, which carries her deep into the interior where she is alone, away from the eyes of neighbours, away from the house she loves despite all its needs. The road is raised up out of the valley, a man-made offering to the gods of industry, and tonight, as on most every night, the road is hers.

When she walks she feels her face hard, her body hard, her muscles elastic and powerful. Her face that is beginning to look like railroad tracks. Well, after thirty-five years in the classroom, what can you expect, she thinks, surrendering her vanities to the wind. Wince never lets Babs talk her looks down. Even when, at the age of forty, she'd had enough of dying her hair and cut it short to let the grey grow in, he refused to let her say she'd aged. That brings a smile to her face now, god love him, my man, she thinks, a hand involuntarily going to the place on her chest where her right breast used to be. And then at forty-seven when she'd had the mastectomy, he wouldn't even let her frown at herself in the mirror. He loved her, he truly did, and he wouldn't let her forget it — even after all these years.

When she walks, she doesn't wear the silicon dummy breast, and sometimes she imagines getting rid of the other breast too, and how then she'd be all flat and hard, though Wince says the hardness is all in her head, says she's soft as dandelion seed to him. Oh Wince, I might really have amounted to something if I hadn't been so well loved. She laughs out loud to catch herself having such a thought. It's true she's been lucky, what with Wince and the girls, beating the cancer, and her job in that town. Thirty-five years teaching, and having only six weeks training when she'd started. That was the way they did it then. She was seventeen, just out of school herself, and when she started there were several grades in the same room. Babs discovered in herself an affinity for organization, planning and communicating, and the students loved her. At least, they made her feel that. In summers, she'd go away to university in the city on bursaries, and by the time she turned twenty-four, she'd earned her teaching certificate. It has been three years since she retired, and now she devotes her evenings to walking. No more planning, no more correcting, no more mediating with parents, mincing through the minefields of school-board politics. The nights were hers for walking. She loved them in a way few others did.

She jumps then, and turns around, recognizing a moment later the slap of beaver tail against the fast, black canal water. It's a funny thing — how she will be shaken by the sounds outside her own head. She doesn't expect them out here; being out here is somehow like being inside herself, so any sound from the natural world is a shock, an intrusion. Babs fills her lungs with the late autumn air. It has started to rain, and the sky will soon find itself bereft of light. She pulls the hood up on her windbreaker. The moodier the weather, the better for her. Fair-weather walkers will be scared inside on such a night. One good blowy day and the leaves will all be gone. Babs sighs and turns her head back to glance down the valley. The valley is perfect for about one week every fall, such a fleeting summit of beauty.

Babs takes notice of the small intake dam on the canal. So she knows she's come about seven kilometres. A long way from home, a long way from anywhere truly, and night is deepening. Well, time to start for home. She ducks through a break in the alder to pee, then starts back in the opposite direction.

Babs knows this road by heart, knows in her body that she must be just over a kilometre from the down turning path. She takes stock; she doesn't feel tired. Her clothes under her water-proof outer layer are wet with sweat. She hears her mother's voice in her head telling her ladies don't sweat; they perspire. Well, Mom, Babs says to the night, I'm the kind of lady who sweats. She pauses for a moment to stretch from side to side; that left hip is giving signs of going out of kilter again. "Oh no," she says aloud. "I must give it a good stretch after my bath." She increases her pace again, pushing hard for the last part. Then she sees him.

All the night hears is her sharp intake of breath, but inside Babs hears herself scream. It's always worse at the end like this, when she's had the whole road to herself all night, when she's given up any thought of seeing someone.

It's the little man with the dog. Mr. Face Full of Shadows, she calls him. Why he would be starting out at this late hour on such a night, Babs can't imagine. There is a moment of tension as they are set to pass one another, the dog growls a little, and his stocky master pulls him close. Babs makes herself look toward his face, preparing for the requisite small town greeting, but he doesn't meet her eyes. The ball cap pulled low over his wide brow hides his face. He passes in silence without admitting her presence in the world and Babs' faint hello perishes on the damp ground.

Goddamn him! she thinks, who does he think he is? Babs knows the man's name, what he does for a living, and that he never had children. She even knows about his wife leaving him for the deputy mayor, yet they've never been introduced. He must know who I am; I've lived my whole life in this town. She mutters her indignation aloud before bursting out laughing. Who cares? she asks the trees. Let it go, girl.

Standing outside her own house, Babs finally takes a moment to rest, to inhale the night from a place of stillness. Through the kitchen window in the front she spies Wince, his balding head still bent over his knitting. A slight babble of radio voices has slipped through those elusive draught seams in their old house, tickling her ear as they pass. There he is, she smiles, knowing by this time he must be nearing the turning of the heel, the reason he knits. My man appreciates the beauty of a well-turned heel, Babs giggles to herself before turning the handle and slipping inside. The intense heat from the woodstove hits her and she begins to undress.

Wince looks up at her over his bifocals. He smiles a crooked smile and the fourth needle drops from his lips to his lap. Babs removes her hikers, goes to him and picks it up. She kisses his mouth before replacing the needle back between his lips. He's counting stitches now; she knows not to interrupt his train of thought. The blare of the provincial radio news follows her down the long hall into the bathroom where a news item stops her cold, freezing her hand's intention to pour a hot bath. She straightens up, steps back out into the hall to better hear . . . *A fifty-one year old woman, viciously assaulted in the middle of the afternoon while walking a popular downtown trail through the capital city . . . this follows a recent rash of sexual assaults . . .* Babs has heard enough, she steps back inside, closes the door, and pours a steeping bath.

I am a woman of ritual, a creature of habit, she says to her lopsided image in the steamed up mirror opposite the tub. And I'm getting old. She loves to soak like this, in her deep cast-iron claw-footed tub. She'll lie in here for an hour sometimes, intermittently replenishing cooler water with hot. Wince knocks gently before entering.

"All these years, Wince, you still ask permission to enter," Babs teases him. Wince, tall and barrel-chested, leans on the counter, his articulate hands gripping the edge of the Formica. He shrugs, "I've never taken my luck for granted." He pushes his glasses farther up on his nose before crossing his arms. "Good walk?"

"Um-hmm." It's on the tip of her tongue to mention her annoyance with the little man, but she changes her mind. "What was that on the news about the woman being assaulted?"

"Lady about your age, in broad daylight, in the middle of town. Some young fellow. They got a good description from her."

"How serious was it? Did they say?"

"Serious enough."

Over the next few days, it seems to Babs that every time she turns on the radio, there is mention of the assault of the female walker, and it is this woman Babs finds herself thinking about as she climbs the hill to the canal. What does she look like? Who was the young man? Why would he be interested in having sex with a woman who was, presumably, more than twice her age? What drove him to such desperation, to attack her in broad daylight? All of these questions occupy Babs on her evening walks, and the most serious consequence to her is that this woman may never again enjoy the simple pleasure of feeling herself independent, a woman moving through the natural world. That she may always fear what danger lurks around the next corner rather than living in the enjoyment of the moment seems to Babs the greatest tragedy of the whole thing, and it is this which she pities. But Babs keeps walking.

This night when she reaches the seven-kilometre mark by the intake dam, she stops suddenly, and slowly turns. She listens; she hears the water moving. It shifts rather than flows — this body of water, pulled by a powerful undertow toward its industrial duty. She hears the odd screech of a blue jay. Most of the songbirds have deserted them by now, as November grows more foreboding. She listens. There is not one sound that reminds her of the town and its houses full of lives. I am far from my house, she thinks, asking herself — who would hear me now? And the thought of the answer makes her cold suddenly, and she quickly changes direction and starts back toward home.

The walking lady moves so fast her feet hardly touch the ground. She is thrilled by this speed, at fifty-five years of age, mother of two, thrilled that she can, but she is ashamed too, ashamed at the reason for the speed. The shame is in this: the thought entered her head that if something like that could happen to a woman her age in the middle of the afternoon, then it is entirely possible that something similar could happen to her — Babs — out here in the dark of night so far from town. Just stop it! she tells herself, but it's no good. The harder she tries to stop thinking about this anonymous woman, the more she sees. The worst thoughts have to do with Babs herself, thoughts she's never given credence to. They have to do with the wisdom of her choices. Things that have been whispered about, she knows, behind her back, having to do with her inviting trouble the way she gallivants around all hours of the night, alone. Why would a woman in her right mind behave that way? She's looking for trouble, that one.

In bed that night, in the dark, holding hands with Wince, her leg flung over his, she asks, "Do you think it's safe — going so far out at night?"

It's a long time before he answers, and she feels his eyes studying her face.

"Do you feel safe?"

And now that he's asked — now that it's out there in the air between them, she knows she must give voice to it. What she wants to say is "Yes, of course! I've spent most of my life in this town. I've never had cause to fear anyone. Who would want to hurt me?" But before the words are out of her mouth her head fills with the words of another answer, and she knows this is the one coming closest to her true feelings. "I'm fit and fast, Wince. I'm strong and I've always wanted to think of myself as being capable of heroics. But if someone wanted to hurt me it would be only too easy to know how and where to do it — everyone knows my habits."

"They do."

"Lots of men of all ages have ATVs that give them quick access to the places I go on foot. Maybe I'm inviting trouble by doing what I do. I walk alone when so many other women walk in pairs. But I need to be alone like that. You know I do."

"I know."

The next night when Babs heads out for her walk, she doesn't notice Wince standing in the kitchen window, watching her go. She is too much taken with making a pact with herself that she will not think about this unknown woman, that she must forgive herself for being unable to do anything about the unjust sufferings of a far away stranger and she mustn't make someone else's troubles her own. It's so damn middle-class, armchair liberal of me to worry about it — it's self-indulgent even, she chastises herself. She forces her attention on external things, remarking on the changing patterns the beavers have made in the river alders along the banks of the canal. She notes the autumn pallet of colours in the larch and the moss and the lichens, how they will change from green to burnt orange, from khaki to mauve to bony white. She thinks, as she always does this time of year, of how beautiful it would be to use those colours in the design of a sweater or a quilt, but she knows it is Wince rather than her who will apply himself to such fanciful creations. Babs remains devoted to her walking. Wince, once he's turned his hand to the creation of a few pairs of wool socks, temporarily slaked his aesthetic thirst for perfectly turned heels, will go back to one of his other passions.

When Wince turned fifty, their daughters gave him a set of Japanese carving chisels. He kept them in the case for two years, taking them out every now and then to admire, but it wasn't until after he and Babs returned from a trip to Europe that he'd begun to use them. The year Babs retired they'd spent three weeks touring central Europe by rail. Out of all the wonderful sights they'd taken in, Wince was most moved by Florence. Especially by the reliefs from *The Singing Gallery* by Donatello in the museum of the Opera Del Duomo. It had been raining that day, and their clothes were damp, but when Wince laid eyes on a frieze depicting many figures of children dancing on an exquisitely ornate balcony, he was awestruck, and ignored Babs' entreaties to go back to the hotel and change. Wince, with his patient attention to detail, had purchased several prints of the panels, and over the last few years had, with his little set of chisels, been painstakingly reproducing the frieze in a great slab of maple. This is something else she loves about him, his quiet determination to find peace through creation.

As the last light wanes in the sky, Babs' attention is drawn to the tips of a stand of black spruce on the far bank. A large murder of crows is gathering. Something is amiss in the world of the crows and Babs imagines for a moment that she can understand their argument. It's over love or politics, she thinks, the only really good arguments are. She pauses, turning toward them, large black-winged figures outlined against a murky sky. She watches them swoop and dive, listens to them bicker and screech. And then she feels it.

A sharp alarm, the rush of blood in her ears, the taste of metal in her mouth. She spins around, sees the dog first, a broad short-legged black thing straining against its chain. At the other end of the chain his master pulls, forcing the dog to give Babs a wide berth. Babs says nothing but stands watching him, waiting for him to look up. The man tilts his face away from her, giving her the view of his puce baseball cap. On his way to the down turning trail, he passes her by without so much as a nod. Babs watches him go, and before she is aware of herself she spits, "FUCKFACE!!" at his retreating figure. But for a split-second hiccup in his stride, the man makes no gesture to indicate he's heard her and continues out of sight. Babs, horrified with herself, claps a gloved hand over her mouth and bolts in the opposite direction.

Babs marches furiously, one hand still covering her mouth, until she finds her knees have begun to shake. She stops, squats down and begins to sob. What is happening to me? she asks herself. She feels her cheeks flush with shame to recall the foul word she'd thrown, weapon-like, at that pathetic little man. She wipes her eyes and stands up, stretches each leg and moves forward again, intending to continue on toward the little dam. She falters, though, for suddenly the night seems to rush in, crowding out the last of the light. She stops to listen. The sounds seem ominous now. Babs finds herself filled with an unspecific panic, and all at once her will to walk deserts her and she turns toward home, thinking only of the safety of her house, with Wince busy inside, and she begins to run.

Panting heavily, and feeling tremendously foolish, Babs reaches her garden. She stops to catch her breath, looks up and meets his eyes. Wince is standing in the front window, curtains drawn carelessly aside, watching her. He knows me, Babs thinks, and then she is weeping and stumbling toward the door. As her hand reaches out for the handle, the door opens and Wince's solid arms are folding her into his embrace.

Wince has her sit down while he removes her walking boots. He pulls her gently to her feet, then lifts her up easily, and carries her through the kitchen and down the hall to their bedroom. With one hand he pulls the blankets back. He lays her down and climbs in beside her. He wraps his arms around her, pulls her close to his chest, and encloses her legs with his. All this he does without speaking. He knows she'll tell him when she's good and ready. They lie like that until sleep comes.

THE PLAYBOY

DEREK CATCHES SIGHT OF HIMSELF IN THE rear view mirror of his rusted powder-blue '89 Ford F150, sizes up his handsome face as he lights a cigarette, guns the engine, and tears out of the soccer field parking lot. It's dark, late on a weeknight, and the young twenty-somethings have been gathering in their ritual end of summer manner — drinking, gossiping, and carrying on. Derek is leaving alone tonight, by choice. He turns his truck away from town, out toward the highway, and cranks the stereo. The Allman Brothers blast into the night, and Derek spits expertly out the window, shaking his head, trying to throw off the mounting irritation building inside him.

"No more chubby, little, brain-dead religious princesses for me!" he whispers into the night. At twenty-four, Derek is the best looking young man in the area, standing at five-feet-eight inches, with piercing blue eyes, untamable dirty-blond, curly hair, and a lean muscled body from his work loading baggage onto planes at the airport. His job pays well, and he knows he should feel lucky to have it. A year ago when he came home looking for work, fresh out of college with his adventure tourism diploma, he had high hopes for a position with the resort. And truly, his training renders him more qualified than any other local. But members of the evangelical church run the resort, like almost all the other major businesses, and they hire their own. So Derek counted his blessings and took a job at the airport. The boss is just a regular Christian from out of town, and doesn't care what religion Derek is, as long as he works hard and shows up on time. The pay is decent, especially since he lives with his parents, and he can fish and paddle in his spare time. But for the absence of a lover capable of keeping his interest, he was doing all right.

Derek pulls off the highway and spins around toward home. He turns down the volume on his stereo as he winds his way through the dark streets of town toward his parents' house; a modest little bungalow set back from the road on a half-acre lot lined with trees. Derek pulls into the driveway and turns off the engine. He sits in his truck for a time, looking out at the property his father had once taken great pride in. The front deck is warping badly; the posts are starting to rot. The paint around the windows is peeling and the siding needs to be scraped and repainted or replaced altogether. The lawn is cut, but Derek himself had attended to that. The woodpile at the back, something his father had always taken great pains to collect and stack neatly early in the season, was barely half its normal size, the logs left uncut in an untidy heap.

Since the old mayor forced his father out of his maintenance job with the town and into early retirement several years ago, he's lost any desire to do much of anything. Several months ago Derek's mother had gone with him into the city to see a doctor and they'd come home with a prescription for Prozac. The mayor has since moved up in the world of politics and is now the provincial representative for the district. The Minister for Stuffed Chicken Breasts, as Derek referred to him, is a big man in the Evangelical church, and the one person Derek blames more than any other for his father's decline.

From the dark front room where his father likely sat in his recliner dozing in and out of sleep, the flickering lights of the TV flash an erratic pattern on the lawn. The old man hadn't even bothered to buy a salmon license this year, and that, to Derek, was the most serious indication that his father is not well. Fishing has been something they'd enjoyed together, just the two of them, for as far back as he could remember. Derek casts a rueful look in the back seat where his rod lies unused inside its case.

"Fundamentalist fucker!" he hisses under his breath.

Derek opens the door and slides out of his truck. He closes it softly, not wanting to wake his mother, and enters the house by the back. He takes his shoes off and walks through the darkened kitchen into the front room where his father lies in his recliner, the lights from the TV flickering across the haggard lines of his face. Derek goes to him and places his hand upon his father's shoulder.

"Dad, go to bed." Getting no response, Derek tries again to rouse him. "Dad, get up, you're drooling on your shirt. Go to bed." Still he does not awaken. Derek shuts off the TV, a natural history program, and it makes him remember how his father used to train sparrows to come and take food from his shoulder. Derek turns away from him, a feeling of disgust in the pit of his stomach, and makes his way down to his bedroom in the basement.

He pulls his shirt off over his head, unbuckles his belt and lets his jeans drop onto the floor. He kicks them out of the way and gets down prone and does fifty push-ups and sixty-five crunches before getting into bed. He lies in the dark, enjoying how the scent of his own body fills the air — the pungent spice of his sweat mingled with the scent of soap on his skin.

There blooms inside him a feeling he is at pains to put words to. At first it presents itself as a nebulous desire to get back at the world for all the unfairness that has affected his family's life. Then, as Derek lies in the dark and focusses on the feeling, it begins to distill itself into a pointed idea to hold someone accountable.

When he wakes the next morning, Derek lurches out of bed with a new sense of purpose. He showers and dresses for work, putting on his favourite jeans, the Calvin Klein's he'd bought from eBay, and turns to admire himself in the mirror. The jeans frame his waist, rear, and legs nicely, displaying his taut figure with tasteful perfection. Derek grabs his wallet, keys, and his new camera phone and bounds up the stairs two at a time into the kitchen where his grey-haired mother sits with her morning coffee, glasses perched on her nose, a cigarette hanging from her lips.

"Mom, I thought you'd quit!" Derek exclaims, grabbing himself a mug and filling his cup.

"Don't say anything please, just let me enjoy myself before school starts."

"What are you doing? What the hell is happening around here?" Derek addresses this last part to the ceiling and sits to wait for his toast to pop.

"I still have two years to go before retirement. You have no idea what it's like — this new principal they've installed — he doesn't even have an education degree. His accent is so thick nobody has a clue what he's saying — and he's teaching math! I'm here with both math and education degrees, but somehow he ends up as my boss telling me how it's going to be! Aw!" she says, swiping the air in front of her as if repelling a horsefly,

"I don't belong to the right club. What can I do but keep my mouth shut?"

She butts out her cigarette and regards her son, "I'm sorry to have to tell you this at your tender age, Derek, but your mother is just a human being, full of flaws, and wrinkles, and regrets."

"Oh, Mom — you're still the best in the West. Is Dad up?" Derek asks, his mother's resigned look over the top of her glasses enough of an answer. "I wish he'd stop taking those pills, Mom, they're sapping the life out of him."

His mother lets out a big sigh and pushes her chair away from the table. "I don't know what to do anymore." She looks at the clock on the microwave, "I've got to get to school. You ready?"

"Yup, just let me brush my teeth."

Derek and his mom drive through town in silence. He pulls into the teacher's entrance of the high school and offers his cheek for her kiss. He watches her make her way toward the building, her handsome figure stooping to the side to counterbalance the heavy weight of her schoolbag.

Derek heads out of the parking lot, using his knees to steer the wheel while he searches for a new disc. He pops in a rare old live Tom Waits recording that he recently downloaded, cranks the volume, and puts his hands back on the wheel. He rolls down the window and hangs his elbow out as he turns onto the highway for the short drive to the airport.

Derek parks in one of the spaces reserved for employees, and enters the little airport terminal by the side door. As he struts past the wickets toward the staff room, he enjoys feeling that both women and men can't help but watch him. He turns to catch the eye of a young woman standing behind the narrow counter of a car rental agency, and before he can pretend to not see her, she waves him over. Derek feels the bitterness of the previous night rise in his belly, admits the disdain he feels for this person, before forcing it down and making himself smile as he walks toward her.

"Hi there, Derek, how are you today?" she asks in a high-pitched voice, leaning toward him over the low counter so that the fat around her middle pushes out evenly around the circumference of her figure, like a child's flotation ring.

Derek suppresses the phrase that comes to mind — "muffin top" — and responds flatly, "Hi, Candy. I'm fine, how are you?"

"So you left early last night — what was your rush, hey?" She tilts her heavily made-up face to the side, the new streaks in her long, permed hair gleaming in the artificial light.

"Oh, I just wanted to get home. I'm right in the middle of this awesome book, and I just can't get it out of my head."

"Oh, yeah?" she asks, suddenly looking uncertain, "What book is it?"

"It's *The Sun Also Rises* by Hemingway. Have you read it?" Okay, now you're just being an asshole, Derek says to himself.

"No, I don't think so," Candy's confidence begins to wane. She puffs out her chest, her ample cleavage aimed at him. "So what's it about?"

"Oh it's about this bunch of Americans, the lost generation, and their travels through Spain after the first world war. They all meet up in Pamplona for the annual fiesta and the bull fights. There's a lot of drinking and fooling around. The main theme, I guess, is about a young man figuring out who he really is."

"Oh, yeah. Right. So, Derek," says Candy, "Have YOU figured out who you really are yet?" She crosses her arms, tucking them in the scant space between her breasts and her potbelly, and begins with one hand to twirl her hair.

"Um . . . What ever do you mean, Candy?" Derek asks.

Candy leans toward him, in a confidential manner, "I'm talking about the only things in life that really matter boy. Babies, marriage, and your own house, of course."

Derek chuckles and cocks his hand, like a gun, at her, "You're too fast for me, Candy." He has her in his sights, pulls the trigger, blows the tip of his finger, turns and walks away.

He changes into the faded imperial-blue work coveralls he'd had his mother alter, and heads out onto the tarmac. He waves to his fellow workers and heads over to where his trolley is parked, catching his image in the large window in the arrival section as he passes.

He picks up his first load from a recently arrived flight, drives across the tarmac to the luggage chute and begins unloading. As he works, he has the feeling of being watched. He tries to ignore it, afraid that it's Candy who is watching him. He turns around and, to his great surprise, finds himself face to face with the very tall and handsome government representative for the district. Well, if it isn't the Minister for Stuffed Chicken Breasts himself, Derek thinks, a broad smile crossing his face as he flashes inwardly on his resolution of the previous night, and the unbelievable luck of meeting the minister today.

Derek smiles and shakes the man's hand. He admires the fine weave of the man's linen suit, as he finds himself agreeing to take him out kayaking the following night. He watches Bruce, as he has been invited to call him, walk away toward the gate by the staff parking lot and for a moment Derek puzzles over the encounter.

The following evening, Derek shows up early at the meeting spot by the old bridge. He wants some time to focus his mind, to reflect on just how he may use the meeting tonight to his advantage. He's thought of little else today. He knows that he has no idea what he's getting into, no plan for how he would like to make the minister for Stuffed Chicken Breasts pay, just clear that he'd like to. Derek lights a cigarette, checks his appearance in the rear view mirror, and sits back to listen to a heavy dub song on his stereo.

Just keep your eyes open and watch for the signs, he says to himself, wait for him to reveal his hand first. I mean what the hell is he doing with me anyway? I'm no church boy. Maybe he wants to convert me. Maybe he just likes me. And with that thought, Derek sees Bruce's spotless silver SUV in his rear-view mirror, a squeaky new fiberglass kayak strapped to the roof rack. He flicks his butt out of the window and gets out to greet the honourable member.

After shaking hands, Derek senses Bruce's insecurity with the boat, and he immediately takes over, easily releasing the tie-downs and lifting the boat down neatly onto the shore. The two get in their boats and Derek leads Bruce across the river, through the deep current, and toward the reeds on the far shore. It would be so easy to tip him out here; the honourable member paddles like a little girl. The damselflies flutter around the pair, one lands on Derek's forearm. He takes notice and blows it gently away.

After paddling their way up a tributary, they pull off at a little spot of exposed shoreline and Derek begins gathering wood for a fire. Bruce stretches out on the sand and watches him carefully. For a moment Derek is seized with panic. He finds himself unable to look in the other man's direction, all the while aware of how he is being studied. What the hell am I doing here with him? Derek demands of himself. He's staring at me like he wants to eat me, for Christ's sake!

Derek forces himself to focus on how his father looked the day he got laid off — like a lost child. He pours the tea with a steady hand and offers a cup to Bruce. He then brazenly lies down beside him. He senses a shift in Bruce, a tensing in the man's body. They each attempt to divine the other's intention. Derek puts down his cup, nestling it in the sand. When Bruce's hand comes down on his buttocks, Derek is stunned, and stares open-mouthed at Bruce. His bottom stings where the other's hand has slapped it with such force that he can feel where each finger connected with his skin.

Derek lies perfectly still for a moment. And then it becomes clear to him. He understands what Bruce is looking for. Derek sits up and smacks the other man hard across the face with the flat of his hand. Bruce cradles his face in his hands as Derek leaps on top of Bruce's prone body, tucks his fingers inside the waistband of his shorts and yanks them roughly down over his potbelly and thighs, exposing the honourable member's fleshy buttocks. Derek lifts his hand high into the air and strikes again and again with all the force in him. Bruce submits to the beating for a moment, his handsome head thrown back, and then he twists with sudden fierceness, throwing Derek off balance. He grabs Derek's arms, jerks him close, and says,

"Let's finish this at my place after dark."

"Yes, Minister," Derek pants.

"You know where to find me?" Bruce asks, releasing Derek's arms, all business now as he gathers his things and makes toward his boat.

"I do."

"I'll leave the garage door unlocked." Bruce pushes his boat into the water, gingerly steps in, and begins paddling down river. Derek covers the fire with sand, checks the shore for anything left behind and slips into his kayak.

Derek returns to his house, the surreality of his situation sinking in. He makes a beeline for his bedroom, calling out a greeting to his father on the way down. Derek lies on his bed for a moment, attempting to focus his mind. His eyes open suddenly and he leaps up, grabs his camera phone, checks the power, and plugs it in. He strips his clothing off and heads to the shower next to his room. He scrubs himself, his skin stinging from the force of the water.

When night has fallen, and the moms have all gathered their children inside, Derek sets out toward the house of The Minister for Stuffed Chicken Breasts. He parks his truck off the side of the road down by the old bridge and continues on foot, skirting the street lamps, imagining himself a ghost. As he approaches the large ranch-style house where his quarry awaits, he stops and pulls out his camera phone, checking the battery power one more time. He slips it back in his pocket and stands across the road from the house. He tells himself that this is it — the only chance he'll have to do this right. He silently crosses the street, approaches the driveway, creeps up to the garage door, and slips his hand into the space left open for him.

THE ARAB

HE EMERGES, ALL BANDY-LEGGED AND CREAKY, OUT of the main door of his home. It's a rusted affair, anchored to the ground by moss tangled through with wild flowers and hop vines. He stands, removes his turban dream hat, and stretches, a mass of knotty grey-white hair falling down behind him.

He waits, his arthritic hands outstretched, filthy fingernails reaching out for contact. And then, as if performing some spell, he kisses the air and the very woods begin to move to his command. The undergrowth dances with new life, the flowers bend and sway to a non-existent wind, and slowly their eyes emerge from the green. Some black, some ginger, others slate grey, calico; they all come whining to him — an army of feline Mongols, and he is the bringer of the feast. They surround him, eddying about his ankles, forcing him to wade through them to reach inside the door and pull out the bag of food. It's the last of it and, as he holds the bag up and tips out the contents, the cats stand on hind legs trying to catch morsels with their front paws, like the raised beggars' hands he barely remembers, so numerous in the city of his birth.

It's the end of the month, and his cheque will be in. The Arab tosses the empty bag over to the great rubbish heap beside the van he calls home. He's lived in the van for many years, ever since he drove it out here after a wild night of poker at the bar. Through some folly he'd have trouble recounting now, he lost his beloved Coupe De Ville, and found himself the owner of this roomy old jalopy. He came out of the bar on Main Street all glassy-eyed, took the thing for a test drive out on the old railway bed, crashed it through the thicket of alder at the side of the trail and landed, happily, in this lovely little clearing. And here he stayed in spite of the best efforts of the good ladies around town to have him moved into the senior's home. He tried that once for a couple of weeks. The meals were good, and the girls were nice, but that's about all he could say for it. They took control of his welfare cheque to pay for his keeping and gave him back less than twenty-five dollars spending money for the month. He could hardly get going in the bar on that amount. So he escaped, and just in time, as the good Christians were planning on having his home towed to the dump.

What would his cats do without him? Anyway, he is meant to be free. It is as his father told him time and time again, paraphrasing the words of the great poet and writer, Khalil Gibran, their fellow countryman who had also come to the new world. He can hear his father's voice whenever he wills, his deep resonant tones still tongued in his native accent.

"Ben, my son," he would say to him, "You are free not when you haven't a care or a worry in the world, but rather you are free when, even in spite of the worries which surround a man, you can rise above them — naked, and open to life."

Ben has always heeded his father's words. He'd made and lost fortunes, this grizzled septuagenarian, and here he is still in the game, still able to ride his bike all the way into town and back, managing on his own under conditions that would make a much younger man crack.

The Arab walks beside his bike, a rusted, old woman's ten-speed, baskets on front and back. Once he turns out onto the old railway bed, following the multicoloured line of electrical extension cords that bring him illegal power from the new split-level at the edge of town, he mounts his steed, and in his slow and steady fashion pedals over the pebble-strewn trail toward the post office where his welfare cheque will most certainly be awaiting his arrival.

On cheque day, Ben's first stop must be the grocery store, because once he hits the bar, chances are he won't leave with a cent left to his name. He leans his bike against the corrugated steel wall and ambles inside. People greet him, calling him Old Ben, and Old Man, and Skipper. Everyone knows him. He understands this is the result of his being something of a "character". Nobody touches him, though, except for his girl. He smiles to think of her, his secret girl, the silent one who saves her sounds for only him.

The Arab cashes his cheque at the counter and buys a large bag of discount cat food, several tins of beans, canned meat, fish, milk, and tea. He manages to fit all of his purchases into the two baskets and walks his bike over to Main Street. He leans it up on the brick window ledge outside the bar, trusting that no one will take his food, and enters the dim room. The barman knows his habits well by now and Ben has only to smile his missing-toothed smile, and lay his money on the counter. The young, shaved-headed barman pours a glass of beer, and exchanges Ben's bills for coins.

Ben takes his place in front of one of the two Video Lottery Terminals, places his glass on the table beside him, and puts his cup of coins on the lip of the machine. The new machines are fixed to eat up bills, but Ben prefers savouring the experience, gets a kick out of hearing the jangling and clinking of coins. He pushes a couple of dollars into the slot and the coloured lights go wild. He enters the trance then, the numb place he visits in the glow of the lights. And as he pumps more of his monthly earnings into the insatiable maw of the VLT, he feels the pressure of *having* seep away. When he gets that cheque cashed every month, the responsibility that money represents weighs on him like a yoke, and it is only when he comes up empty after a day of pumping and drinking that his soul feels light.

Some hours later, when the bills have all been changed, and all the change fed to the machine, Ben stands up, swaying a little on account of the beer. He staggers out onto the sidewalk, shielding his eyes from the glare of the sun, and stumbles over to his bike. She's been here — his girl. He can smell her spearmint-scented skin, wood-smoke hair. He can't help but smile at the magic of it; how she exists like a shadow in the town, only becoming flesh and sound in his bed.

He knows it is too soon to ask his old body to carry him home, so Ben walks his bike down Main Street a ways, to the bench on the side of the road, and sits staring across at the empty lot. This is ritual for him. He sits here under the foggy spell of the beer, remembering the cinema his father built after so many years of toil, and how the people came from miles around to see the moving pictures his father brought in from faraway places. They were treasured then, his father and he, for offering the people of the woods a window into the greater world. They were like magicians. And after the trials his father had endured because of his brown skin and his strange accent, because of his attempting to do business outside the graces of the company that owned the town, it was such sweet success to feel the people's gratitude. The townspeople could call him The Arab. They didn't know anything about the world, and his father didn't really care what anyone called him. They needed him, and in the end that was what mattered.

Ben closes his eyes and imagines he is sitting in the back row of the Roxy. He remembers the squeak of vinyl against his bare leg during the annual two-week heat wave. He remembers, too, the tang of bodies crowded in for the premiere of *Gone With The Wind*, and how the damp mothers shushed and rocked their children to sleep, praying for some peace while they watched the lush story play out. They'd never seen anything like the genteel world of Scarlet O'Hara. Their fingers were sticky with spruce sap and their boots encrusted with the fetid mud of these uncultivated streets carved out of wilderness. These dark-skinned foreigners had offered them a beauty they'd never known. Ben and his father had lived in a small flat next to the projection room; the cinema was their life. And then one night the place went up in flames, the Roxy was burned to the ground, and all that was left was this empty lot. That's what killed his father, Ben thinks, he couldn't start all over again. Ben lifts his hat and bows his head at the empty weed-spattered place where his father once lived.

Knowing his body is ready now, Ben makes himself stand up, takes the handles of his bike in his leathered fingers and commences pushing toward home. He walks his bike up the short hill to the old railway bed before he attempts to mount it, weaving for a moment like a flag in the wind until he straightens out and pedals in a slow and even rhythm along the trail toward his home. Some are amazed by this old man, how he can ferry himself and his heavy supplies so far on that rusted heap of metal with his brain swimming in alcohol, his old eyes yellow and bloodshot.

He pedals a long way over the rocky path, his dusty shoes separating at the sides, and he does not pause, knowing his cats will be awaiting his arrival. He reaches the edge of the town, and as he passes by the new house with the grey siding, its owner appears around the corner, their eyes meeting for a moment. Ben is aware of the man's contempt for him, a contempt he tries to conceal behind the requisite small-town nod, but it exists in the sudden stiffness of his middle-aged body, in the social climbing desires of his newly paved driveway, and in the suspicious way he follows Ben with his eyes as he struggles on toward his place beyond the tracks. Ben smiles to himself, wondering how long it will be before the man discovers the extension cord plugged into the outdoor socket at the side of his new shed.

When he reaches the narrow path leading from the trail to his clearing, The Arab summons the little energy he has left, gets off his bike and holds on as it rolls downhill toward his home, the perfumed alder leaves brushing his face. Exhausted, he lets the bike fall, the contents of the baskets spilling onto the ground, and stumbles inside. He collapses, fully dressed on his bed, and passes out.

Some time later, through the fog of his sleep, he hears the ebbing and flowing of sound, almost like music but more animal, like an ancient prehistoric song sung by a being with no tongue, and he knows she is here. She who searches without finding, the only person to grace his doorstep and, though he cannot open his eyes, he sends his love to her, his girl. He falls deep into sleep again, helpless to defend himself against the power of it. The weight of alcohol joins with the heaviness of fatigue from this life lived so close to the bone, and he sleeps like one dead.

And then, in the swollen dark of night, the world explodes. The first thing that reaches Ben, reaches into the depth of his sleep, is the stench of burning hair, and it is a moment before he snaps to attention, bolts upright in his bed, and realizes his own hair is burning. He runs an arthritic hand over the back of his head, squeezing out the flame, his leathery skin hardly admitting the pain of the heat. His eyes fully open then, to the horror of his home engulfed in flames and the unearthly screeching of cats. Ben leaps up from his bed, arms thrust out, trying to find the doorway. He comes full stop against the door, closed for the first time that summer, and as the van begins to melt with the heat, the flames devouring the last of the oxygen, Ben blasts the door with all the force his old body can summon and it gives way with a rusty groan. He tumbles out into the night, rolling onto the ground and crawling as far from the heat as he is able. He lies down on the moss, gathering a singed cat to his chest. As he watches the flames devour his home, he thinks of his father, and of the words of Khalil Gibran, and he closes his eyes.

SPIDER GIRL

ONE BOOTED FOOT IN FRONT OF THE other, she creeps slowly through town, her mp3 player plugged into her ears, large violet eyes peering out from under the frizzy brown fringe of her long hair. She makes her way to the graveyard, to the Catholic side where her father is buried, and sits in the woody grass next to his modest granite stone, the high swooping voice of Kate Bush giving the whole scene an other worldly intensity.

She crosses her legs, no longer an easy task in her tight bell-bottomed jeans, the excess fat around her middle squeezing out over the top of her waistband. It wasn't always like this. Her body remembers a time of lightness, a time of cartwheels and climbing, a time when she weighed so little it seemed the wind could pick her up and blow her away. Now there is heaviness, the ground is no longer steady beneath her feet, her body a strange lumbering thing, and her father preparing for his second winter underground.

Daisy plucks out three long stalks of grass, and pinching the ends under her boot, she braids them together, the stalks kinking at odd angles as her agile fingers force them into submission. She places the first braid over her father's stone and makes another and another in varying lengths and thicknesses, until the letters of her father's name are hidden beneath the ropes of grass. She then arranges them in quirky concentric shapes radiating out to the edge of the stone. The effect is like a large green spider's web. Satisfied with her work, she stands, turns, and begins to make her creeping way to where her mother and little sister await her. When she reaches the front step of their government-owned row house, Daisy pauses and looks up. The narrow three-story house seems to scrape the sky.

As she passes over the threshold, Daisy's nostrils fill with the scent of her mother's reheating. Her mother does not cook anything fresh, at least not often. Most of their meals are ready-made purchases from the recesses of the large deep freezers of the local grocery store. The crispy grease-soaked, meat-like lumps taste like faded memories of food, like wispy dreams of the things they once were. Chicken, codfish, beef, and pork, all ground up, diluted, breaded, watered, soaked, flattened, fattened, and nuggetfied.

Daisy hangs up her faded jean jacket with the skull and crossed bones appliqué on the back, and bends to untie her boots, the effort of this activity making her dizzy. She rights herself, holding the wall for support, pulls her earphones out, and enters the small front room. Her sister, Stacy, sits on the bare tile floor, her tiny body curled in a ball watching Sponge Bob on the wide-screen TV. Daisy stands for a moment looking at her, wondering how it is that as she grows ever larger, her sister seems to be shrinking. Stacy turns and catches sight of her,

"Hi, Daisy. Where were you? You know what? I was the helper today and I got to lead the whole class to the gym and then I got to write my name on the board with Miss' special marker, you know the black smooth one that smells kinda squeaky but I couldn't do all the letters myself 'specially not the "y" and Miss said to ask you to help me so can you, huh?"

"Whoa — slow down speedy — I just got in the door." Daisy smiles at her sister, "You know how to do a "y" — what, did you get nervous and forget?"

"Yeah, I sink so. But I have to practice my name every night."

"Okay, so let's eat first and then we'll do it, all right?"

This seems to pacify Stacy who turns back to her show. Daisy returns to the hall then enters the kitchen. Her mother sits at the table as if frozen, staring out the adjacent window at the tall grass of the narrow, fenced backyard.

Daisy stands for a moment, waiting for her mother to notice her. Her mother's long hair is greasy and pulled back in a tight ponytail. Three inches of grey span from the roots outward where, in a severe line, the colour changes to a purplish brown. My mother was never a great beauty, Daisy thinks, but there was a time when she looked a lot better than this. Hanging on the wall, just over her mother's shoulder, Daisy catches sight of her father's smiling face. And then, without meaning to, the memories of the afternoon her father died come rushing in, hitting her with raw natural force, like a tidal wave, making her feel small and helpless under the weight of it. And the worst part of it to Daisy is that she never saw it coming. She'd been twelve years old and had been unaware that her father's behaviour leading up to that day had been anything but normal and adult and appropriate. Her cheeks burn with shame to admit this: she should have known there was something wrong with him.

"Hi, Daisy. Supper's in the oven — can you dish it out please?" Her mother's voice startles her and for a brief second

Daisy doesn't know where she is, and then she turns from the photograph, gathers the plates and cutlery, and begins laying out the evening meal.

Later, after she has cleared the dishes, sat with Stacy to help her print her name, and completed the bare minimum of her own homework, Daisy retreats to her room on the top floor and locks the door. She steps over discarded clothing, half-read books and magazines, and sits at her desk. She turns on her computer, and as she waits for it to boot up, takes a deep breath. As she exhales, it feels as if all the dross of the day flows out of her. All the nasty looks and snide remarks from the perfectly turned out girls in their expensive jeans and top-of-the-line jackets.

Daisy logs into her favourite chat room.

"Are you alone?" he asks as soon as she enters.

"Yes. I'm always alone here."

"Good. I don't want to share you with anyone. What are you wearing right now?"

"Nothing special. A black lace bustier with garters attached. Black stockings . . . no panties."

"That's nice. Bend over will you? I want to see your bum. Tell me what it looks like."

"It's perfect. Heart shaped, small yet ample at the same time. My skin is creamy white and smooth."

"That's perfect. Where are you?"

"I'm lying on a reclining chair on the balcony off the top floor of my beach house. It's sunny, there's a warm breeze, and I can see the sand from here. It's almost white, and the sea . . . it's so blue."

"That sounds so good. Tell me — Where is your house?"

"I can't tell you that."

"Why not?"

"Superheroes must keep their identity secret. I'm in the last place you'd ever expect to find me."

"But I do want to find you."

"Maybe we've already met."

"I don't think so, Spider Girl. Will you at least consider meeting me somewhere — anywhere?"

"I'll think about it. I'm going in now. Night is coming and I have work to do."

"All right. Think about me, will you?"

"I will."

Daisy crawls over the tangled bedclothes to get into her bed, pulling at the button on her jeans to release her skin from its confinement. She lies on her back, her right hand travelling down the swollen path of her belly to her cleft where her fingers reach between the secret folds of flesh and with quick light caresses she brings herself to orgasm. She rests for a moment, her eyes closed, then goes again, imagining the smooth, strong, hard body of her lover pressing against her, running his fingers over her flat belly, between her slim thighs.

While Daisy sleeps in her teenaged cocoon, Spider Girl is awake and roaming, patrolling the dark dream world in search of Daisy's father. She slips unnoticed through the dingy pub on Main Street where the coloured lights from the VLT machines cast lewd shadows on the strange patrons. The old Arab with his laughing eyes and his knotty hair winks in her direction, as if he sees what others do not. Spider Girl casts webs on the walls and the late night drinkers and the misfits fall into her traps. But she cannot find the man she seeks. Spider Girl leaves the bar, and shooting webs out of her wrists, swings from lamp to lamp along the Main Street. She cuts through the trees, making her way to the industrial wasteland on the outskirts of town, a growing feeling of dread in her belly, her spider sense telling her something is terribly wrong.

As she approaches the fenced-in yard where the school buses are put to sleep each night, she retracts her webs and continues on foot, her dread increasing with each dark step. Her heightened sense of smell tells her he is here before she sees him. The sickly sweet reek of rum hits her, and she turns her head in revulsion. Her night vision aids her to pick out, first the shiny bald patch atop his head, and then the outline of his body, his small pot-bellied frame slumped against the side of his school bus, his long, thin hair falling from just the sides of his head over his shoulders, an empty bottle of dark rum overturned at his side.

As Spider Girl approaches she realizes with horror that the school bus is still full of children. She forces the door open and takes the steps in a single bound. The children, very young ones, about Stacy's age, are sleeping, their heads on each other's laps and shoulders, their bags open, the floor littered with empty wrappers that look as if they have been licked clean. Spider Girl spins the largest web of her career, one large enough to encompass all the sleeping children, and using all her super strength, she pushes the roof off the bus, and sends it flying into the yard, opposite to where her father lies. She gathers the web of children on her back and, shooting chains of webs from her wrists, she swings through the streets of town, delivering each of the children to their homes, hoping with her superhero hope that she can do the impossible — return all the children without their parents coming to realize the terrible transgression of her father. As the last child is returned to her bed, Spider Girl wilts with fatigue, and by the time she returns to the yard to retrieve her sleeping father, she is incapable of producing any more web. She attempts to rouse him, to make him walk home of his own accord, but he will not be roused. Too weak to lift him, Spider Girl knows she must leave him before she is discovered. She begins to make her way home before first light, knowing he will soon be discovered, knowing she has failed. She returns to her beach house, and falls into a deep, profoundly exhausted sleep.

At school the next day, Daisy slouches from class to class, trying to make herself invisible. She attempts to focus on what the teachers are saying, but inevitably her concentration wanes and she finds herself daydreaming about Spider Girl's beach house, and about how wonderful it would be if she could open her eyes and find herself transported there.

Her last class of the day, her favourite, is English Literature with Mr. Wand. The subject of the lesson is the short story. They have read several stories in class over the last couple of weeks, and now the students are asked to write their own. Although Daisy offers nothing to the discussion, she pays close attention. Mr. Wand is a small, quiet man the students like to call Velcro behind his back, because he keeps his hands stuck in his pockets. He is all business related to the subject he is teaching, doesn't acknowledge jokes, refuses to be sidetracked, a grey bland-looking man. Daisy, though, has seen him smile on occasion when his back is turned to the class. She senses something lurking underneath his everyman appearance and, for this reason, feels a kind of complicity with him. In his class she makes her best effort to write intelligently. Before the bell rings, Daisy begins scribbling notes for an outline for her story, the same one that seems to have been writing itself in her head for some time. She gathers her things and files out of the class, attempting a glance at Mr. Wand as she shuffles past. Her teacher, seemingly oblivious to her presence, turns back to his desk, picks up a book by some foreign author Daisy doesn't recognize, and begins reading.

That evening, upon arriving home, Daisy finds her sister outside playing hopscotch with a friend, and her mother asleep on the couch. Daisy watches her mother, her face creased with a tension that sleep has not eased. Daisy quietly picks up a tattered patchwork quilt, opens it out and lays it over her sleeping mother. She goes into the kitchen, opens the freezer, pulls out a box of fish sticks and a half bag of French fries and turns on the oven. While she waits for the oven to heat up, she sits down at her mother's place at the table and looks out the window. The tall grass has faded from green to light brown, and soon will be covered in snow. Daisy kneels on the chair, forces open the window, leans out as far as she can without falling, reaches out her hands and yanks out several fistfuls of long stalks. She pulls them inside and closes the window.

As Daisy reheats the evening meal, she works on another web, this one quirkier than the last owing to the tougher nature of the medium, its refusal to bend smoothly. She works quickly, her dexterous fingers shaping the interconnected web, feeling something close to panic rise in her; a fear that her mother will wake before her web is complete. Her fingers fly with a nimble agility that the rest of her body can only dream of. As the timer bell goes to signal that the fish sticks are ready, Daisy completes her project. She lifts the baking sheet out of the oven and lays it on the stove. She takes her strange web and tiptoes into the front room, places the web over the blanketed form of her sleeping mother, and turns to go and find her sister.

Daisy and Stacy sit in the kitchen to eat their dinner, Stacy chatting incessantly about her day, Daisy patiently listening.

Then, in mid-sentence, Stacy drops her fork onto her plate and looks up, her eyes welling with tears.

"What is it?" Daisy asks. Stacy cannot speak, only shakes her head as tears spill down her face.

"Come on now Stacy, you have to tell me. What's wrong?"

"Don't get mad," Stacy whispers, eyes cast down toward the puddle of ketchup on her plate.

"I'm not going to get mad. Will you please tell me?"

"Okay," Stacy says, her voice barely audible, "but I don't want HER to hear." She nods her head in the direction of the living room where their mother still sleeps.

"She's asleep, just tell me already!"

"You know Jesse, right — grade three Jesse?"

"Oh yeah — the little pipsqueak in the last house on the row. What about him?"

Stacy takes a deep breath, and bursts into tears. She struggles to speak quietly, the words coming out in fits and starts.

"He said my dad was a — you know — a person who gets drunk. And he said that he was a — " At this point Stacy covers her face with her hands and sobs into them, making spluttering sounds in her efforts to contain her distress.

"What else did that little fucker say?" Daisy gently pulls Stacy's hands away from her face.

Stacy looks at her sister incredulously. "You said the F word Daisy."

"I'm sorry, Stacy, but I was mad. Now I want to hear what else he said." Stacy, seemingly calm now, looks at her sister, her eyes wide. "He said that Dad could have killed all those kids in the bus and then he would have been a murderer on top of being a — you know — drunk and that was the reason for why he had the accident."

"Oh, yeah? Well, Stacy, don't listen to Jesse Hutchings. He's so ugly he never even had a father. When he was born his father took one look at him and left him alone with his ugly, fat mother. He's a stupid jerk, so don't talk to him any more, okay? Don't even look at him, all right?"

"Okay," Stacy agrees, at once cheerful again. "Anyway he stinks, right?" She looks to her sister for approval, her face full of glee.

"That's right, Stacy — he stinks."

Daisy catches sight of her rumpled mother standing in the doorway. She smiles weakly and slides down into the chair that Daisy normally sits in.

"Who stinks?"

"Oh, just Stacy's gym teacher at the end of the class," Daisy quickly improvises, catching Stacy's eye. "Right, Stacy?"

"Yup, he sure stinks!" Stacy laughs and Daisy gets up to serve her mother dinner.

That evening, after her mother and sister have settled in their own rooms for the night, Daisy locks her door and logs on to her computer. Her friend is waiting for her in the chat room.

"I missed you."

"Did you really?" Spider Girl answers.

"Sure I did. I've been thinking about you all day. I was thinking that perhaps you are really younger than you pretend to be?"

"Is that what you think?"

"Yes. It's all right though, I don't mind. I just want you to know its okay with me."

"How young would you like me to be?" Spider Girl asks. There is a moment of silence, and Daisy can almost hear him hesitating.

"Too young to bleed."

Daisy stares at the screen, too shocked to know how to respond. She pauses, her fingers poised over the keyboards, as it suddenly occurs to her: Stacy is too young to bleed. This realization fills her with revulsion. What have I been playing at?

"Fuck off, pervert."

Daisy logs off before allowing him to respond. She throws herself on her bed and buries her face in the blankets. What fun have I got left now? she asks herself. Her answer comes: Spider Girl. She grabs her notes from her schoolbag and begins her story in the middle.

When Spider Girl awakes, it is with the sour realization that she has failed her father. She leaps out of bed, her muscles aching with fatigue. She looks at the clock: it's late in the afternoon. Surely, she thinks, they have discovered him by now. She dons her sleek black Spider Girl suit, secures her straight shiny locks under her headpiece, and heads out to find him. She sticks to the shadows and the trails, avoiding the main streets. She refrains from spinning webs; she must not be seen. When she comes to the yard where the school bus had been the previous night, she does not see her father, only the overturned empty rum bottle abandoned under the bus. Spider Girl stops for a moment, thinking. She turns around and makes her silent way back toward town, slipping unseen into each of the local drinking establishments in search for him. It finally occurs to her that he may be at home by now and she makes her way, still travelling in shadow, to the side of town where the untidy government row houses are, with the paint peeling off the pickets of the narrow, fenced gardens.

Spider Girl, her senses filling with dread, skirts around the back of the row of houses, and climbing through the woods behind them, comes to the one where he lives. A figure on the roof catches her eye and for a moment her heart lifts with joy to see him standing with a large brush in his hands, a bucket of tar at his side, and him working away, his long hair fluttering in the wind, seemingly oblivious to the fact that a few hours before he'd gone to work drunk and almost caused the death of a busload of little schoolchildren. But before Spider Girl can ask herself how it could be that he was not yet in police custody, she hears the sirens blaring, and sees her father look up from his work. Neighbours come rushing out of their houses, looking up and pointing at him. The sirens come closer, and her father, appearing dumbfounded, as if he has no idea what all the fuss is about, loses his precarious footing. For a brief second, it seems to Spider Girl that time stops as her father's eyes meet hers, him on the rooftop, her in the trees at the back of the property, and before she can make a move to save him, he tumbles off the roof and falls, with a dull thud, onto the ground three stories below. Her mother comes screaming out of the back door and runs to him. Spider Girl shrinks back into the trees, knowing that she has come too late.

At school a few days later, Daisy delays leaving the English class, placing herself at the end of the line of students handing in their short stories to Mr. Wand. As the boy in front of her leaves, Daisy refrains from moving any closer to the teacher. He looks up from his seat at the desk, and holds out his hand, a bland expression on his face. Daisy flips her story toward him, its title "Spider Girl" clearly visible on the front page. She steps closer and places it in his outstretched hand. Mr. Wand stares at the title for a moment, a strange expression clouding his features, and looks up at her.

"Thank you, Daisy." He croaks, his voice dry and rough.

"You're welcome, sir," Daisy mumbles.

That night, Daisy dreams of Spider Girl in her house on the beach. Fatigued from a night of patrolling the dark streets, defending the ones who need her protection, she has fallen asleep downstairs on the couch in front of the TV. Unbeknownst to her, a storm rages outside, the waves begin to pound at the walls of her house again and again. At last the water forms itself into a great wall and crashes over the house, bursting through the windows and flooding the rooms.

In the black of night, Daisy wakes with a start, bolting out of bed, her breath fast and panicked. The sound of heavy rain pounding on the roof is unbelievably loud. Daisy is freezing cold; her body begins to shiver. She finds that she is soaking wet, her nightdress clinging to her distended belly, and she doesn't know what is happening. She leans over and feels her bedclothes, finding them drenched. She lifts her wet hands to her nose, wondering with disbelief whether she herself has wet the bed, yet the smell is not one of urine, but rather a musty, mildewy odour. And then she hears it: drip, drip, drip. She looks up to the ceiling above her bed, sees the wide crack in the plaster, and the water dripping heavily down, falling with a flat thud on the sodden bed. Daisy stands there, paralyzed for a moment, wondering what to do. And then a weird low keening issues forth from her mouth, the force of it welling up from deep inside her, and now she knows, with a terrible certainty, that she is alone in the world with no superhero to come to her rescue.

The Committee Lady

MADELINE CALLAHAN SHUTS THE DOOR OF HER sturdy bungalow at exactly eight thirty-five on this Tuesday morning. She bustles down the narrow street, crowded on either side with small multi-coloured houses, toward the town centre where the other committee members for The Foundation for the Preservation of Historical Buildings will soon convene. With her portfolio of information tucked under her arm, her stout little sixty-one-year-old body waddles intently toward her destination.

The Committee Lady has, for many years, involved herself in the running of the town, but after the death of her husband five years previous, she has immersed herself in her volunteer work. With her children grown and her husband gone, there were none of the usual familial commitments and restraints to prevent her from joining every committee in existence, as well as creating a few of her own. There was much work to be done. Her self-imposed frantic schedule has kept her so busy these last years, that occasionally it will occur to her days have passed since she has paid any heed at all to the memory of her late husband Horace.

She trundles along, barely cognizant of the fierce wind tearing at her clothing, so focussed is she on her destination. This particular committee's life has reached the point when it must be taken by the horns and steered in a focussed, logical direction.

She walks along Main Street, on the only sidewalk in town, pausing for a moment to stare at the dark mirrored window of the bar, a thorn in her side if there ever was one. "Hand a thorn in the side of the 'ole town has well — though people hare too hignorant to see it," she mumbles this last bit out loud.

"If I live to see the day liquor is banned from this town — I will not have lived in vain," she says to herself, her eye falling upon one such ruined person pedalling along on his battered bicycle. He approaches, his wiry body stubbornly forcing itself to carry him upright regardless of the degree to which he's chosen to pollute it.

"Hello, my dear!" she calls out in greeting to him, squaring her shoulders and jutting her chin out, her dry pale lips tensing in preparation for the encounter.

"How are you today, Ben? Still up and about I see!" she says brightly, not giving him a chance to respond. He stops his bike and places his feet on solid ground "Now Ben. When are you going to let me help you get back into the home? I heard that old van of yours got all burnt up."

"Oh, Missus," grins Old Ben, his purple tongue showing through the hole in his smile. "You know I can't stand to be locked up like a creature in a cage."

"No one wants to lock you up, Ben, we just want you to be looked after properly, that's all."

"You're special," he allows, tipping his hat that reminds Madeline of a turban at her, and continues on his inevitable way toward the bar.

Madeline turns for a moment, watching him pedal off in his slow yet effective manner, finds herself shaking her head in disapproval as he dismounts in front of that place of badness, then the wind picks up and the sand on the sidewalk dances and swirls around Ben's ankles as he disappears into the dark building. For a brief moment she has the sense of the world widening before her, of the landscape opening up like a colossal mouth, one full of different peoples in different lands living in ways she has never even come close to imagining, so immense this flash of vision that she feels her own self begin to disappear. And then the great mouth closes, and the world is once again this desolate little main street and she the only inhabitant in this god forsaken place with the interest and intention to make things right. Her moment of insight gone like a seed in the wind, she turns and charges on toward her destination.

The meeting today is being held in the offices of the honourable member for the district, a Mr. Bruce Hancock, in the only brick building in town, this singularity of aesthetic not being lost on Madeline. She is the first to arrive, and quickly arranges the chairs appropriately, taking her handkerchief from her sleeve and dusting the chair and place at the table which will be occupied by the honourable member. She tucks the hanky back in its place and, glancing at the door, wishes to confirm that no one has witnessed her display of devotion.

As Madeline busies herself with the preparation of the coffee and tea, the other members arrive in ones and twos. She greets each of them by name and begins handing round her minutes from the last meeting. Seven of the committee members have arrived and, as they take their seats, they make the kind of small talk ubiquitous in small towns all over — on the subject of the weather primarily, as well as a brief but unsatisfactory foray into the scandalous behaviour of young people. Unsatisfactory because there is not one among them who is able to suggest a solution to the timeless problem. Madeline remains quiet during the disjointed conversation, awaiting the arrival of the honourable member who acts as chair for this particular committee.

At last he breezes in, tall, almost lean, and very elegantly dressed, his whiting hair beautifully cut, his blue eyes smiling out from above his chiseled features as he makes a charming self-effacing apology for his tardiness. As she watches him, Madeline feels her body rise from her seat and reach toward him, feels herself flush with an intense yearning, a deep and powerful urge that she can only identify with her religion, with the desire to be touched, nay *filled* with the holy spirit. Madeline censors herself immediately, returning to her seat and inadvertently knocking her notes off the table. As she moves to collect them, she struggles to make her face a mask of normality. She forces down the tumult of feeling making itself known to her and, reeling with confusion, attempts to normalize her thoughts, and steer the meeting toward an effective direction.

The rest of the brief meeting passes like a blur for Madeline until she realizes the members are discussing the upcoming fundraiser.

"Perhaps we could approach all the businesses on Main Street to donate items for an auction," she finds herself suggesting. The honourable member ties things up quickly, assuring Madeline of his confidence in her abilities. As he breezes out of the room, leaving an awed silence in his wake, Madeline becomes aware of a long-suppressed suspicion. She now admits to herself a feeling of resentment toward him for his ability to make it seem as though he is actually contributing his efforts in a meaningful way to the necessary work of the committee.

As the committee members prepare to depart, Madeline tidies the room, making vacuous conversation, moving and adjusting chairs unnecessarily. She puts on her coat, for although it's only late summer the wind is fierce, gathers her things, and waits for the others to file out. She takes her key, stops in the doorway to turn out the light, and regards the room for a moment, a feeling of embarrassment overcoming her as she notes the wetness in her woman parts. She extinguishes the light, locks the door, and hurries out, hoping to avoid conversation with anyone.

As Madeline begins to turn back toward Main Street, she hesitates and, instead of heading toward her home, indulges a rare whim to walk to the beach.

She follows the sidewalk along Main Street as it slopes down toward the water. The wind caresses her light-brown, beauty salon-tinted hair, and she just barely resists the urge to skip. As she crosses over the rough path that runs parallel above the red sand beach, like a giant sickle, it is her late husband Horace that her mind now falls upon. Something is weighing upon her conscience, just out of her reach and, as she recalls the fading memory of her late husband's face, she grasps the tail end of the thing and attempts to yank it into focus and articulate it to herself before it slips away. The feeling she'd experienced at the meeting, the one that has left her thrumming with a restless energy — well the terrible thing is this: she can't recall ever having felt anything like that for Horace. Sure she'd loved him and had been, as far as she could tell, a dutiful wife and faithful companion. But this other thing — the loving physical part — here Madeline stops on the spongy root-crossed path and steadies herself by grasping the weeping perfumed trunk of a black spruce. Well, the thing was it had left her feeling cold in her insides and slightly — here she asks for God's forgiveness — repulsed. And that, Madeline shakes her head, breathing deeply of the violent air, is surely as sinful as Old Ben and his drink. What right have I, she wonders, to tell other people how they should live?

She straightens up and continues on the path around the lake, her hand sticky now with sap, and her heart heavy with the admission that she hadn't enjoyed her marriage in her body, that she'd never known any feeling in her body for a man that came anything close to what she'd felt today for Bruce Hancock. And that, thinks Madeline, is so extremely inappropriate. She picks up her pace, pushing her short legs to increase their stride.

Suddenly, Madeline hears a strange, guttural sound coming from the direction of the water. She stops in her tracks, and listens, the sound rising in its intensity. Madeline wonders what bird, what animal could be the mistress of such a voice, and as her curiosity compels her, she moves as quietly as possible toward the sound. She bends and ducks under branches, her portfolio secured awkwardly under her arm. She, much to her own surprise, gets down on her hands and knees to crawl through the underbrush to where there is a break in the trees. Here she glimpses the figure of a human being in all its unclothed glory swaying in the breeze. Madeline freezes just behind the edge of underbrush, still on her hands and knees, her portfolio, unbeknownst to her, fallen on the decaying leaf strewn earth. The creature she spies is one that has been known to Madeline for many years, yet never in this naked form, and never making sound. This person, known to everyone in town as a mute half-breed, a wandering idiot girl-woman, stands with her arms raised, hips rocking side to side, her long lean young body performing some subtle swaying dance as if to beckon the wind to come and caress her naked form. Watching her, Madeline feels a sharp stab of envy.

Madeline lurches back on her heels, making the branches rustle and crack as she does so. The girl cocks her head toward the sound, her body perfectly still for a moment, before she quickly pulls on her clothes and darts over the sand toward the town, disappearing from sight.

Watching her go, Madeline's eyes swell with tears, her chest heaves, and an involuntary cry flies from her mouth. She lurches out of the brush and onto the path. She straightens up, wipes her eyes, brushes the front of her trousers off, and makes her way home.

After two strange nights alone in her house, her evenings spent sitting in the dark in her front room, the silence unbroken by anything electronic, Madeline awakens the next morning with a determination to confront this welling inside her. She bathes, taking more care than usual with the styling of her hair. She fetches her makeup bag out of the linen cupboard, where it has sat unused since the death of Horace, and takes great care applying liner and mascara to her eyes. She draws a rouge-tipped brush across her cheeks, and covers her lips with a red tinted balm. She begins to dress, digging out pantyhose from the bottom of her underwear drawer, donning a full slip and a merlot-coloured, knee-length belted dress. She finds a pair of black pumps in the back of her closet, and puts them on, her feet wincing a little, unaccustomed as they are to anything but the most sensible flat shoes. She takes a hat the she hasn't worn in more than twenty years down from the shelf and, looking in the mirror, places it on her head. The grey wool cloche style suits her well. She dons her long Sunday, black wool coat, and ties it snugly around her not-so-slim waist. She stops for a still moment to appraise herself in the mirror. "I've never been what you'd call beautiful," she says without a trace of self-pity, "but I do look handsome like this." And with that thought she opens the front door and steps out into the world.

Madeline gets into her car, a well-maintained, ten-year-old silver Chevy Lumina, starts it up, and pulls out of the drive. She advances through the town in a safe and steady manner toward his house on the other side of the lake, all the while taking deep calming breaths, assuring herself that her purpose is only to test her own emotions in his presence, not to make an advance that could only be refused to her great humiliation.

When she reaches his house, she pulls to the opposite side of the road, and shuts off the engine. She sits for a moment, composing her thoughts — some ideas for relevant questions relating to the approaching fundraiser — then opens the door and proceeds to cross the quiet street. Madeline draws up to the heavy storm door of the large, ranch-style house. She raises her hand to press the doorbell and a curious, rather pleasant peace descends upon her.

When she rings the doorbell, it seems to Madeline that the sound is incongruously loud, echoing through the house as if it were empty. She stands listening for an approaching step. She looks at his SUV in the driveway, at the partly open garage door, and rings the doorbell again. This time she hears, as if from deep underground, a strange muffled sound; the sound of a creature wishing to make itself known to her, but unable to circumvent the barriers of language and door. Her instinct tells her the sound is a beckoning one, and for a moment she stands paralyzed, wondering what to do.

"Bruce, are you there?" She calls out, deciding to address him by his first name — since she is his senior after all. "Bruce, it's Madeline. I've come to settle a few things about the fundraiser." Again the strange noise. Madeline realizes with a shock that the sound is human and she knocks again on the door, raising her voice in alarm, "Bruce, it's Madeline. I'm going to let myself in." She tries the handle, and to her relief, finds it open.

She steps into the white foyer, her pumps tapping on the tile floor. She closes the door and turns, suddenly overcome with shyness, and calls out to him, her voice sounding to herself almost feeble. "Bruce, it's Madeline — are you here?"

She hears the sound with great clarity now, the pained muffled sounds of a man in distress. Madeline takes a deep breath,

"Bruce, I'm coming to help."

She moves through the house toward him, her shoes tapping on the floor, the sharp sound an odd counterpoint to his moaning. She moves through the kitchen and dining room, both painted white, the appliances sparkling stainless steel. As she steps into the white-carpeted living room, the light is very dim. Heavy-duty white drapes have been pulled across the windows and Madeline squints in an effort to see. After several seconds, her eyes adjust to the dim light and she sees him. He is crouched on the ground, his back to her, his long, once athletic body completely naked. His mouth is gagged with a dark piece of fabric. Ropes bind his wrists to the pipe extending from the large cast iron radiator beneath the far window.

He turns his head, casting her a desperate look over his shoulder. Madeline turns to the large, plush sectional sofa and grabs a soft, red throw blanket. Averting her eyes from his naked state, and wishing to preserve his dignity, she opens the blanket into a large, draping rectangle and places it around his shoulders, her tender hands pressing the fabric onto him. He slumps toward the floor. Madeline reaches over him and makes eye contact. She uses both hands to gently pull the cloth out of his mouth.

He hangs his head, "Thank you," he says hoarsely. She refrains from asking him any questions, believing this the best way to show her respect, and moves her hands to the rope binding his wrists to the radiator. After a futile minute trying to untie the knots, she says in a low voice, "I'll have to do this with a knife; won't be a moment." And she moves to the kitchen, pausing to take account of the room and, guessing correctly, finds the cutlery drawer on the first attempt. She chooses a small steak knife and moves back over to the man slumped beneath the red blanket. As she works on cutting the ropes, Madeline finds herself struggling to remain focussed on the delicate task in front of her, finds herself almost overwhelmed by the powerful masculine animal scent coming off him. It's been years since she has been so close to a man like this, in such an intimate way, and as she worries the edge of the knife back and forth across the rough surface of the rope she takes deep breaths, and moves in close to him. The scent of him makes her feel light-headed, and she nearly loses her grip on the knife. At last the rope gives way, and Madeline places the knife on the floor and hurries to free his wrists. She takes hold of his arms to examine where the rope has chaffed the skin before slowly releasing him.

"Oh Bruce, my dear man, who did this to you?" she asks, her arms flying around his shoulders and pressing him into a warm embrace. She feels his arms around her back returning her gesture with a light pressure, and Madeline hangs onto him until he pulls her arms away.

"You must promise me you'll never tell anyone about this," he whispers, his hot breath tickling her ear.

"How can you say that? We must call the police — you've been tortured, your home violated, your — " he grabs her shoulders and moves his head in front of hers until they sit awkwardly, face to face, on the floor. "You must never speak of this, Madeline — my position depends upon it. Do you understand me? Can I put my faith in you?" Madeline hangs her head, and inadvertently sees his body exposed before her, the red blanket having fallen from his shoulders, his belly just obscuring his private parts. She reaches out her hands and looks into his eyes, wanting now to give him anything he desires. She whispers, "Of course, you can trust me. I'll never betray your trust, Bruce."

"Thank you, Madeline." He nods, and giving her shoulder a friendly squeeze, he pulls the blanket about him, covers himself and stands. "I'm going to shower and dress now," he says casually as he walks away from her, leaving her splayed ungracefully in her merlot dress.

Madeline struggles to her feet. She raises a hand to her cheek, feeling the skin hot to her touch. She takes a deep breath and smoothes her dress. Her hands are moist and she stands for a moment, waiting for her pulse to slow.

"Tea, that's what we need." she says. Madeline bustles about the kitchen, poking through perfectly arranged cupboards to find the necessary components of a civilized tea. She arranges the dishes on the large white marble-top table and sits, awaiting his return.

When he strides into the room, beautifully cleaned and dressed in a deep-blue, long-sleeved silk shirt and well-cut, tan linen trousers, smelling of expensive cologne, he looks at the dishes, and says, "Oh, sorry Madeline, I haven't any time for that. I should have been at the office twenty minutes ago. Can I drop you anywhere?" he asks.

With a sharp intake of breath, Madeline freezes for a second as he leaves. She follows him, and knowing she has been dismissed, she forces her voice to respond nonchalantly. "No, thank you, I've got my car with me today." She stands up and walks as smartly as she can toward the front door where he waits holding it open. As she leaves the house, she hears the door close, a dull smack like a fist hitting a face. Before she can turn to look at him, to reassure herself that what she thinks happened did indeed occur, he has already climbed into his SUV and closed the door. As she walks toward her car on the other side of the street, willing her body to remain composed, she hears him call out to her. "I suppose you had some information for me regarding the fundraiser. You can just leave it at my office with Brenda. Bye, now!" He waves as he pulls out of the driveway. Madeline stands alone beside her car, her fingers fumbling with the buttons on her good Sunday coat.

The Housewife

Sharon Jenkins watches her youngest child's chest rise and fall as she surrenders finally to the sleep her mother has prayed might come. The two older boys are long since collapsed from exhaustion after the busy day at school, the walk home through snow-covered streets, and the weekly session of karate held at the local legion. Sharon creeps out of her toddler's bedroom, leaving the door slightly ajar, and tiptoes down the long hall to the living room where she collapses on the brown leatherette sofa.

Too tired even to turn on the lamp beside her, Sharon tries to force her brain to wade through the fog of her weariness and focus on doing something constructive with these rare quiet moments when she is able to hear herself think without the cacophony of children. Her gaze settles on the window where the curtains have yet to be drawn. The dim light from the street lamp reaches through heavily falling snow into her living room, and puddles on the new laminate floor. She hears the muted roar of a truck's engine and, before the headlights have a chance to impose themselves upon her solitude, she is sitting up and moving to the window. She hides her slim frame behind the red polyester drape and peers out, guiltily trying for a glimpse of him as he climbs out of his truck and makes his way through the snow. He grabs the blue scoop abandoned on the bottom step of the house by his father, who gave up on trying to stay ahead of the furious drifts and had gone in to wait out the storm. Was it her imagination or did the young man cast a look in her direction? Sharon watches as he works, speedily clearing the heavy bank of snow. She allows herself to imagine him without his winter clothes, as he looked in the summer, lean and blond, skin browned from working outside, a body that inspired fantasy. And fantasy is all she's had for much of these last years, since her husband went off to work in the oil patch, returning every six weeks for three weeks at home. After the joy of reuniting had worn away there'd be the awkward struggles for dominance in the household, and then the ever-increasing tension as the time for leaving would approach once again.

They came to think of her husband's overseas job as necessary — as so many others did. It paid for their renovated house, their new pickup truck, their skidoo, ATV, and various other toys, and most importantly it allowed Sharon to remain at home with the children. The very idea of that being a luxury made her laugh. Staying at home had been, so far, the hardest, most unrelenting job of her thirty-five years.

Now he carves a path through the snow to the house. He stops, cupping his hands and curling his back to protect his flame from the wind, and lights a cigarette. Then he saunters out to the end of the drive, facing the window she is looking out of. He takes a long draw on his smoke. Sharon, slightly ashamed of herself, but unwilling to move from her spot at the window, tries to supplant the man in front of her with the image of her husband. So sweet and good-natured, almost child-like in his simplistic approach to life, her Chris is a warm and decent husband and a good father. Yet he isn't here. And he's been absent so much of the last years that, to Sharon, he's begun to seem almost unreal.

Sharon steps out in front of the curtain into the window and yanks the elastic band out of her long brown hair. She turns toward the faux antique floor lamp, puts the light on, and tossing her thin tresses over her shoulder, faces the window once again. She makes as if she is watching the storm, craning her neck to regard the snowbanks in an exaggerated fashion, like an actor in an amateur theatrical production. She sneaks a look in his direction — he seems to stare into space, oblivious to her existence. As Sharon spies the young man, willing him to notice her, she experiences a chill down deep in her gut. He seems to stare straight toward her. At that moment a gust of wind tears through their little street, picking up the top layer of loose snow and scattering it through the air in an erratic fashion. She shivers, pulls her cardigan about her shoulders, as the young man turns and disappears into the night. Sharon remembers with a start that she's forgotten to stoke the wood stove.

"Damn it!" she says to no one in particular. Chris has had to ask her on several occasions to please mind her mouth around the children, and she was doing her best to oblige. But the truth is, admits Sharon with a tilt of her chin, she enjoys the sound of her own inappropriate language. She jogs down the stairs to the rec room and opens the door to the wood stove to find the fire barely smouldering. "Goddamit! As if I don't have enough to do around here!" she mutters to herself as she goes about chopping splits. The struggle to keep the fire burning hot enough to prevent downdrafts filling her house with smoke on severely windy days was wearing Sharon down. They'd installed the woodstove to mitigate the rising cost of home heating oil, and the heat was wonderful. Yet it had kept her so busy running up and down stairs half the day, tending to the fire and bringing in wood from the stacks Chris had made in the shed, that she'd barely had time to enjoy it. And now hearing the wind howl on nights like this filled Sharon with dread, something she'd kept herself from confessing to her husband, knowing he needed to see her as highly competent, able to look after the house as well as the children as he laboured so far away in the oil camps.

Sharon squats on a large junk of wood as she nurses the fire. She feels the pricking of a splinter on her bottom and she lifts her weight to remove it. Her worn jogging pants are too large, and her red v-neck sweater is smeared with cheese sauce left by little hands. She gazes into the fire remembering the way she'd taken such pride in her appearance before she'd had children. When she met Chris, she was a saleswoman at the top car dealership in the city, the only woman on the floor. She wore wrap dresses and pencil skirts, figure-hugging outfits that had shown off her good looks. Plenty of men had noticed her. Then, after she got pregnant, they moved out here, to the town where Chris had grown up. It made sense at the time, but then he'd had to go away to work, and Sharon was left to spend her winters virtually alone in this isolated place. It seems impossible now, like a dream. The idea of walking into work, back into that showroom, that place of masculine ferocity, vicious competition, now filled her with anxiety. I couldn't do that now, she thinks. I've lost my guts.

Sharon feeds the fire and closes the furnace door. She stands up, her back muscles a tangle of knots, and climbs the stairs. She returns to the living room window to find the street barely visible through the swirling snow. She draws the curtains and flops down once more on her sofa. Idly wondering what to do with the few precious hours stretching out before her like an untravelled highway, the desire for a drink suddenly presents itself to her and, before her mother-self has a chance to talk her out of it, she is moving toward the little kitchen and hopping up onto the Formica counter top. She reaches back into the top cupboard behind the children's fever medication for the bottle of Glenlivet she has kept on hand ever since Amber was weaned. Scotch was something the boys at the dealership had introduced her to. Bottle in hand, she hops down onto the laminate floor, and gets herself a large wine glass, fills it with ice, and pours a generous portion of scotch on top. Before she leaves the room, she grabs a clean, red tea towel out of the drawer, covers the bottle, and pushes it to the back of the counter.

Holding her glass up high and to the side, as if it's a dance partner's hand, Sharon saunters into the living room and deposits herself and her drink at the pressed wood desk in the corner where her computer resides. Checking her e-mail she finds a message entitled "missing you all" from Chris. She opens the message, but soon finds her attention waning while reading his rather lackluster descriptions of camp life, his references to men whose names mean nothing to her. Sharon closes the e-mail, telling herself she'll read it later in the morning after the boys are at school and Amber is having her hour of TV time.

She takes a long drink of scotch, and sits staring at the glass for a moment, savouring the burning sensation in her throat, and then the warm glow in the pit of her stomach. She raises her glass, "I love this stuff," she says out loud, hopping up and peering round the corner to the hallway as the sound of her voice cuts through the silence of the house.

Sharon turns back to her computer and takes another sip of scotch. She clicks on the search engine and types a website address into the box. She'd committed the address to memory the night before when she heard it discussed in an investigative journalism show on the subject of voyeurism. It had seemed almost offensive to her at the time; how people could offer their most intimate selves up to public viewing. But now, tonight, in this rare idle moment, Sharon admits her curiosity. She feels the looming darkness of loneliness threatening to cover her, and so she reaches out with her fingertips to enter the words that will give her entrance to another world.

It takes Sharon's eyes a moment to adjust to the slightly blurry, slightly slowed down quality of the webcam picture. As she turns up the volume on her computer, she hears the strains of cello music coming from another room. Sharon watches for a moment, taking in details of the space. The webcam is set above a large bed covered in richly textured silver-coloured fabric. The wall behind is painted a cool Venetian Blue, a beautifully upholstered Queen Anne chair flanks the bed, and this is about all she can see in detail. It's as if Sharon is transformed into a fly and has landed on the ceiling of a bedroom from another time. Sharon hears the sound of a woman's voice approaching. A slender female arm slips into view as she pulls down the duvet and slides her body into the bed. Her hair is long and dark, and she is beautiful; an olive-skinned Mediterranean beauty that seems to fit perfectly with her surroundings. She lifts her arms and stretches prettily, as if she is unaware of the camera. As the woman lies waiting, Sharon wonders how many other people like her in rooms all over the world are watching through the eyes of this fly on the ceiling.

After a time, Sharon hears the sound of footsteps approaching, and the woman's face lights up with a smile as she pulls the covers open and another figure slides into the bed. Before Sharon can glimpse a look at the face of the new person, they are embracing passionately. The new figure has short, light-brown hair and, when they pull apart for a moment, the duvet falls down a little to reveal two pairs of breasts, and Sharon realizes with a start that she is watching two women together. Sharon brings her hand to her lips, in silent shock, and is about to turn away, but she doesn't. She reaches for her glass of scotch and takes a drink.

The women smile at each other, and Sharon notices that the new one is attractive too, in a tomboyish way. They make no indication that they are aware of being watched, so Sharon relaxes a little, telling herself it's like a lovely moving painting, not pornography. The women begin to kiss slowly, their hands caressing one another's shoulders and backs and breasts. They begin to moan and writhe, the duvet falls away completely, and as the short-haired woman pulls away to gently push her lover back onto the bed and lowers herself to kiss her breasts, Sharon feels herself stirring.

As the woman on top kisses her way down her lover's body, Sharon brings a hand up over her eyes. Yet she cannot turn away as the woman opens her lover's legs and brings her face close to lick and kiss her secret places. Sharon watches with one eye as the long-haired woman receives this attention greedily. She moans and twists, she pulls the hair of her friend; she caresses her own breasts, her tongue licking her own lips. Sharon begins to ache, her eyes have filled up and her breathing grows deep and fast. As the dark-haired woman's sounds and writhing become more intense, Sharon begins to sweat, unable to turn her eyes away. When the dark-haired woman comes, she lets out a peal of ecstasy and before her cry is extinguished, Sharon reaches out her hand and shuts the window.

Sharon closes her eyes and waits for her breathing to slow. She listens for any sound outside herself, but all she can hear is the muted hum of the refrigerator. The silence is so heavy, so pervasive, that Sharon has the image of herself and her little house with her sleeping children inside as an island in a sea of snow.

She drains her glass of scotch and lets an ice cube fall into her mouth, chewing until it melts and slips down her throat. This will be the last drink until Chris gets home she says to herself, wiping her damp forehead with the back of her hand. She finds that she is perspiring, taxed from an exertion that is so frustratingly mental. Sharon looks toward her bedroom, a feeling of dread coming over her; the idea of entering that room alone again. And then she hears it: the sound of his truck starting up.

Before Sharon can censure herself, she leaps up and dashes out to the front porch where her winter clothes hang on hooks. She pushes her feet into her long boots, pulling them up over her legs, throws her coat over her shoulders, opens the door and tears out into the storm. Through the haze of blowing snow she sees him raking the shovel across the end of the drive in front of his truck. As he sticks the shovel in the snow bank and turns to climb in, Sharon struggles through the deep drifts that have invaded her driveway, and makes her way toward him. He starts the truck and pulls out into the road just as Sharon herself steps out of the snow bank and into the street. She moves toward his truck as he pulls up alongside her. Sharon raises her hand in greeting. The truck stops, and Sharon grasps the handle of his door and opens it up. He smiles in surprise at her. Sharon opens her mouth to speak, but she suddenly becomes aware of the recklessness of her behaviour, and all she can think of to say is, "Hi."

"Hi," he says, "What a night, hey?"

"Yeah, it's wild," she says, feeling her cheeks burning, and desperately searching for a reason to have stopped him.

"You all right over there?" he asks after an awkward silence.

"Oh, yeah, it's just —" Sharon grasps the first excuse which comes to mind, "The power's been going on and off all night. I was wondering if you had the same trouble."

"No, none." He says, his eyes flicking to the snow blowing into his truck.

"Okay, just thought I'd ask," Sharon blurts, "Good night." She slams the door of his truck and runs back into her house. His eyes follow her for a moment, a puzzled expression on his pretty face. He guns the engine and disappears out of sight.

Sharon enters the hallway, locks the door, and hangs up her clothes. Tears well up in her eyes and she places her cold fingers over them and breathes, forcing back the need to cry. She goes to the desk and shuts the computer down, picks up her scotch glass and takes it into the kitchen. She washes the glass, takes the tea towel off the bottle of scotch and puts the bottle back into the cupboard. She pours herself a glass of water, takes two aspirin, and drinks it down.

Sharon moves through the house, first stoking the fire one last time, then turning out lights. She opens the door to her boys' bedroom to find them sleeping peacefully. She stands in the doorway to her daughter's room, listens to the sound of her breathing, and resists the urge to go to her. She slips into her own bed, checking to make sure her alarm is set for the early hour when she will rise and attend to the needs of her children, the day a series of extinguishing little fires and stoking larger ones, running from one to another until the late dark hour when she will again find herself lying in a heap of exhaustion alone on the couch in her living room.

Don Wand

LIFTING UP THE BED-SKIRT, HE REACHES ONE long hairy arm underneath and grasps the sacred object. There are no dust bunnies to scatter at his touch; everything in his house is clean and polished. He takes the satin-lined box — which used to contain the Bible his mother gave him when he graduated university — and sits on the bed. He places the box on his lap and, pushing his glasses up onto the bridge of his nose, lays both hands upon it. Then, as if performing a sacred ritual, he removes the cover and holds it aloft for a moment before laying it down beside him. He bows his head, hunching over to get close enough to see the contents.

Inside there are a myriad of tiny lower jawbones with the teeth intact. Each bone holds a long incisor at the front, and behind the little space, called, he knows, the diastema, there are three molars. All of these have been painstakingly collected and bleached, gathered together like the bones of venerated prophets. Don Wand, high school teacher, church leader, only child, and sole caregiver to an aging and sometimes overbearing mother, gently fingers the little teeth. His mouth falls open, his eyes glisten with moisture as he places the left lower jawbone complete with teeth in the centre of his palm.

Barely able to feel the weight, Don closes his eyes, takes a deep breath, and holds it in, his body perfectly still.

"Donald! Don! What are you doing in there?"

"I need to have my footbath dear, fill it up for me now will you?" Don Wand expels his breath in a slow and controlled manner, like a singer. "Just a minute, I'll be right out!" He does his best to keep the annoyance out of his voice. He replaces the bone in the box and returns it to its hiding place under the bed. He stands up, all five-foot-four of him, and heads out to the living room where his mother waits in her relining chair in front of the large-screen TV.

"What were you doing in there, all on your own?" she eyes him suspiciously.

"None of your damn business, you old bat!" he wants to say, but does not. "Just doing a little research online, something for school," he says.

"Well, at least it's good for something, that old hinternet. Some says there's an awful lot of odd stuff going on in that, some evil business and whatnot." Barely listening to her, Don goes about retrieving and filling her footbath. He carries it over to her, places it on the floor, and helps her off with her slippers and socks. He must work to hide his disgust of her old woman's body. She's never been one to exercise, and it shows. Her toenails are thick and wooden, growing in every direction, and the smell of her woman parts, from down here on the floor in front of her, makes him want to retch.

Once a girl passes out of puberty into womanhood, her sweetness transforms into something sinister and frightening, her smells go from sweet to acrid, and the difference between the two is so dramatic, like the difference between a mermaid and a gorgon. Don Wand should know. He teaches them at a time when the change is palpable. They come to him, most of them still too young to bleed, the scent of youth emanating so flagrantly off their taut little girl bodies. Their gaze is so open and trusting and curious, the undamaged ones, the ones from good Christian homes at least. And then the changes begin; their faces close to him, a veil of suspicion falls over their eyes, which they make to seem vacant, the bleeding starts, and he can smell the change in them.

Don Wand pats his mother's leg and rises.

"I'm going out for my walk now. You'll be all right on your own for a couple of hours, won't you?"

His mother looks sharply up at him; her faded hazel eyes magnified by thick glasses.

"Where do you have to go now? It'll be dark soon."

"It won't be dark for a few hours yet, mother. I've got to stay fit, don't I? Someone has to be strong enough to look after you in your old age, don't they?" He rises, smiling, and gives her shoulder a pat. "Good night now, and don't forget to take your feet out of the water after Coronation Street, okay?" He turns toward the door, neatly evading her question of his destination for the evening.

Don Wand sets out, a pair of surgical gloves thrust deep in the pocket of his track pants. He climbs into his pickup truck — a new, oversized, navy Dodge Ram — looking over his shoulder to check that his walking stick is still in the back where he left it the last time. He drives out of town, nodding to a neighbour as he goes, turns onto the highway and accelerates, heading toward the low lying mountains on the other side of the lake. After several kilometres, he turns off the highway onto a dirt road and rolls down the window, the smell from the district incinerator hitting him with its intensely unpleasant fragrance as he draws closer to the dump.

The wire gate is locked, the regular worker having left for the evening, but this does not deter Don Wand. He drives past the dump for a half-kilometre and parks his truck just off the road behind a small stand of birch at the edge of a large cutover. He gets out, walking stick in hand. He makes his way back toward the dump, his five-foot-five wooden staff held aloft, imagining himself as the prophet Moses. The stick, stripped of its bark, sanded and stained, has a "y" at one end with a nail protruding down from the centre. It had been a tricky procedure, figuring out how to create just the perfect tool for his purposes, filing that nail down to make it sharp at both ends, and sinking it into place.

Don Wand throws his stick over the chain-link fence, then climbs over and drops lightly to the ground on the other side. He picks up his staff, imagining himself as Nimrod, the great hunter from the book of Genesis. He holds it aloft like a spear and moves in a stealthy manner toward the incinerator. He circles behind it, knowing his quarry will keep a safe distance from the heat and, as he moves, his heart begins to race a little. He approaches the other side, where the garbage will fall sometimes from the great height of the incinerator bridge when the trucks back in to unburden themselves. What falls is free picking. He waits, making like a statue, until they begin to show themselves. Large and filthy, bodies slicked with grease, covered with toxic soot that rains all around them from the ever-burning incinerator, their pink hairless tails give them up. Don Wand, with the patience of Job himself, waits until they accept his presence as they would a stone, and when one crosses his path, a long slinky one with bits of fur missing, he brings his stick down with the wrath of the old testament God himself and catches the thing on the flank, pressing the nail through its little body as the rat flails desperately. Death does not come fast enough, but the head must not be damaged, and so he leans with both arms on his stick, watching and waiting until the tenacious little thing finally expires.

He lifts up his weapon then, and holding it slightly raised in front of him, heads away from the heat toward the outer limits of the dumping grounds. He reaches the edge of the trees, grabs a fallen branch and pries his kill loose from the nail. He gathers rocks from near the site and covers the body well. Decomposition takes much longer this way, but at least another animal won't carry it off. Don bows his head for a moment before standing. He removes the surgical gloves from his pocket and squeezes his hands into them. He begins to explore the older section of his burial ground, turning over rocks until he hits pay dirt — a neatly decomposed corpse with little more than the bones and bits of fur remaining. He kneels, and laying down his stick, begins to pry the lower jawbone loose from the skeleton, the bones cracking easily beneath the strength of his short sturdy fingers. He separates the two halves from the connecting ligament and examines the teeth for a moment — yellowed molars slightly chipped but a complete set nonetheless. Don Wand is pleased. He inverts the glove on his right hand, enclosing the two halves of the lower jawbone within, and holding the precious item in one hand and his staff in the other, begins his journey home.

Darkness is just beginning to close in on the split-level house, and Don enters quietly, listening for her. He hears the sound of a laugh track coming from the TV in her bedroom, and slips down the hall to his own room before she catches sight of him. He keeps a little corner in his room ready for this particular work, and this is where he goes with his treasure. He puts on a pair of yellow rubber gloves, pours hydrogen peroxide and water together into a mid-sized mason jar, drops the jawbones in and screws on a lid. He places the jar into a box, and pushes it far back on the floor under his computer desk. He puts everything neatly away and goes to clean himself thoroughly before visiting his mother to say good night.

Don Wand turns off the lights in the kitchen and living room. He locks the doors and sets the timer on the coffee pot. He enters his room and closes the door, enjoying the feeling of privacy now that his mother sleeps and several dark rooms separate them. He sits at his computer, his legs tucked under his chair, and checks his work e-mail, answering a few necessary ones, making sure he is ready for the coming workday.

Finally Don Wand logs into a chat room, one he'd found after overhearing a couple of young girls discussing it in the hallway, and spends a few moments reading the text for the last hour or so, wanting to know who has been in this evening. He seeks the company of one person in particular, someone who goes by the tag "Spider Girl". They'd been enjoying a harmless flirtation for the last while, and Don Wand was curious as to how far things could go. He enters his tagline "Exterminator".

"Are you there, Spider Girl?"

No response from Spider Girl, just a few idiotic comments from a couple of other participants. Don Wand ignores them. She's different, the one he seeks, she's not given to silly conversation either. He tries again.

"Are you lurking in here, waiting for me to find you? Why don't you show yourself?"

No response from her. He's got to be more forthright to draw her out, he thinks. She wants a strong man. She wants someone to take charge, to lead her. "Good night, then, Spider Girl, I haven't got time to hang around waiting." And then he has her.

"Wait, please — I'm here. I need your company tonight. I'm not myself. Just stay for a bit, okay?"

Exterminator moves his chair closer to the keyboard. He must play her like a virtuoso now, must make her offer what she wants to give him. He welcomes her into a private chat. She accepts.

"I sense a need in you, Spider Girl. What are you feeling tonight?"

"I feel all alone in the world. Like I'm surrounded by people, but completely alone in my own head."

"I know exactly what you mean, I feel the same thing. Like nobody knows me, they have an idea of me, and that's what I give them. Yet all the while I'm living another existence unseen by everyone around me."

"That's it! You've said it for me! How can that be? Are you really out there somewhere, Exterminator?"

He pauses a moment before responding. His level of excitement has risen to such a pitch, he must roll his chair back from the desk to give room to his swelling erection. "I'm really here Spider Girl. Now stand up and come over to me . . . Are you doing it?"

A hesitation from Spider Girl. "I am."

"Good. Now turn and let me see you. Tell me, what sort of panties are you wearing?"

"Pink cotton, with a little frill at the edge."

"Perfect." Exterminator closes his eyes, touching himself. "I'm putting my hands on you now, Spider Girl, my big hands are running up your thighs, my fingers are so long they are covering your whole perfect bottom. I'm pressing my face into you. You smell so good, so young. Can you feel me?"

"Yes."

"Sweet. Just let me smell you for a moment." Exterminator pushes his chair back, grabs himself and pulls ferociously for a few seconds until he releases all over the front of his track pants. He opens his eyes, pushes his chair back and jumps up. He strips down and wipes his hand off in his pants. He hops erratically for a moment, looking around, wondering what to do first. He dashes to the door and opens it, peering into the darkness before scurrying down the hall to the bathroom. He drops his pants into the laundry hamper and washes his hands before returning to his room.

"Spider Girl? Are you still there?"

"I thought you'd gone."

"No — Just recovering. You drive me crazy."

"Good. I've got to go. Work to do and all that."

"All right. Until tomorrow?"

"Yes. Good night."

"Good night."

Don Wand shuts down his computer, and with a smug smile gracing his rather nondescript features, he takes off his glasses and gets down to his evening ritual of deep breathing before turning in for the night.

At school the next day he gives his class the week's assignment, a short story, and sits behind his desk, pretending to work as they begin notes for story ideas. He watches them when they aren't looking, especially the girls. A few of them are still on the sweet side of girlhood, and these he loves best, knowing the sweetness won't last long. Some of them have already crossed over and he tries to keep his gaze from lingering on them, knowing they will scowl if they happen to catch his eye.

Don Wand zeros in on a plump girl with long brown hair obscuring her features. She bends over her notes, scribbling.

She looks up, catches his eye, doesn't scowl, but holds his gaze. Don Wand is the first to look away. Her father's death and reprehensible behaviour prior to the event a couple of years ago have worked their troubled details into the town's lore, become changed into legend by gossiping women.

After school, Don Wand hops in his truck and just as he is about to turn the key to start it up, he notices a yellow envelope on the passenger seat. He picks it up and reads the words scrawled in a childish hand on the front: "For Don Wand's eyes only." Don looks around the parking lot, wondering whether he is being watched, thinking perhaps some students are playing a prank, but nobody seems to be paying him the least attention. He opens the envelope, and finding only a disc, puts it aside and starts up his truck.

Don drives the quarter kilometre down to his church, The Everlasting Church of the Evangelical. He grabs his folder of financial statements and enters the first door to the right of the main entrance. Two other members of the church's financial committee are already seated, both women, both retired from their jobs and active members of the various committees. They smile and greet Don Wand as he enters. Don sits at the head of the table, a fitting place for the treasurer, and keeps his head in his papers rather than make small talk. Finally, nine and a half minutes late, the last member of the committee enters. Bruce Hancock, Honorable Member for the district and the newly minted Minister of Municipal Affairs. The two women actually rise to greet him when he enters and Don, too, finds himself rising to shake the honourable member's hand.

As they buckle down to the afternoon's work, Don takes the floor, giving his opinion of the state of the church's finances, the rate and frequency of tithing from the various families, and upcoming fundraising projects. Don delivers his carefully compiled numbers to the committee, but as he speaks, his gaze keeps returning to Bruce Hancock who sits, smiling toward him, his face a mask of attention, but behind the eyes, Don thinks, he is somewhere else. Don Wand, realizing the honourable member only pretends to listen, bristles with indignation, his palms begin to sweat, the skin atop his balding head begins to itch, and so overcome with a sudden fury is he that it is all he can do to keep his voice steady, his words clear and even. Don is filled with a rush of hatred toward this man, with his easy good looks, his full head of hair and his polished charm, and while he finishes reading the end of his statement in a dry and dull voice, his soul rages with resentment.

When Don finishes, Bruce Hancock smiles at him, extends his well-manicured hand, and congratulates him on a job well done. Don, forcing a smile, accepts the gesture, making small talk as he gathers his things and leaves the church.

Don Wand gets into his truck, placing his briefcase carefully on the floor of the passenger's side. The yellow envelope sits on the seat. As the pastor leaves the church he waves at him and Don responds with a wave of his own, muttering "phony fucker" under his breath. When he arrives at the well-paved driveway of his own house, Don gathers his things, along with the mysterious disc, and goes inside.

At home his mother waits for him on her chair in the living room, calling out to him as soon as she hears the door crack.

"You're late today, Donald. I was expecting you at three-thirty."

Don takes a deep breath through his nose before he answers. "I had the meeting at the church, I mentioned that this morning, Mother."

"Did you? I don't remember you saying anything. Well, what odds, you're here now. Would you get me a cup of tea, my dear?"

"I will, if you'd just give me a minute to get in the door!" Don snaps at her and a look of shock crosses her slack features.

"There's no need to take that tone with me, young man, is there?"

"No, I don't suppose there is," Don mutters, passing her by as he moves toward his room, "I'll get the tea in a few minutes."

Don closes the door and places his briefcase beside his desk. He sits in front of his computer and inserts the disc. After a few moments of fiddling, trying to find the right program with which to play it, Don views the video.

At first, Don is not sure what he is looking at, but as his eyes adjust to the scene before him, he sees quite clearly the kneeling figure of a man. Don starts as he realizes the man is completely naked. Although the sound quality is poor, Don Wand's ears begin to decipher the dialogue between the man on screen and the one behind it.

"So, now I want you to tell me why you invited me here," says the rather young-sounding man's voice from behind the camera. There is a moment of silence as the camera eyes the naked form of the man on the floor. The man's wrists are tied with rope to the pipe extending from an old fashioned radiator. His back is to the camera. In the silence he slips the rope along the pipe down toward the floor and spreads his hands, bringing himself onto his knees, lifting his bottom so that he is completely exposed to the man with the camera.

"Why did you invite me here?" the videographer asks.

"I wanted to . . . " The rest of the sentence is unclear.

"Say it louder for me."

"I wanted to be with you." The man's head full of whitening hair falls with this confession, and Don Wand recognizes Bruce Hancock's voice as the voice of the naked man on the screen. Don brings his hands up to his head in an expression of disbelief as he watches the camera move in closer on the flabby figure of the naked man.

"Ask me nicely and I'll give you what you want," whispers the voice behind the lens as he moves around the man.

"Give me a spanking . . . please," he repeats, turning his head toward the man who now stands above and to the side of him, the expression on his handsome face changing from supplication to horror as he sees the camera phone pointed at him and he understands for the first time that he is being filmed. As Don Wand watches the man struggle and curse his captor, the screen goes black, and Don sits staring, his mouth hanging open in disbelief.

His first reaction is outrage. How could a man debase himself in such a manner? And not just any man, he thinks, but one of the leaders of our church, a minister of government, someone responsible for the well being of others. Don feels a rush of nausea rise in him and he stands, pacing his room, taking deep breaths as he waits for it to pass.

Someone did this thing and chose to give it to me, Don thinks. He wonders what he should do with this information. Who left it for him and why? Don Wand ejects the disc from his hard drive, replacing it in the case and hiding it in the box with the jar of bleaching bones, pushing it far back against the wall under the desk and out of sight.

A week passes. Don watches those around him, looking for something in someone's eye that might hint at knowledge of this mysterious intrusion into his life. He detects no change in anyone's behaviour. Don Wand looks after his mother, he teaches his students, he goes to church, takes walks at the dump and chats online. He waits.

His students line up to hand in their short story assignments. They barely acknowledge each other; he mutters a thank you to each of them as they file out of the room. Don Wand leans over the side of his desk, reaching for his briefcase, thinking they have all left, thinking his work is finished for the day when he sees her. Plump face partially obscured by untamed brown hair, she regards him with one violet eye. He is taken aback at her expression. Not jaded, edgy, as he would have expected from her, but open, curious. Don Wand finds himself smiling as he accepts her paper. He looks down at the title page, the letters bold and artistic, printed in a Gothic font, "SPIDER GIRL". He goes very still. He looks up at her, unable to breathe. She smiles with half of her mouth, looks at him for a second before turning on her heel and walking out of the room.

Don Wand takes the paper, and with unsteady hands, deposits it inside his briefcase. He walks quickly out of the school to his truck. He drives straight to the dump, passing by the still-open gates and parks in his habitual spot behind the little stand of birch. He opens the window and sits in the silence of his truck, waiting for the panic in his bloodstream to quell, waiting to feel himself again. After a time, his breathing normalizes, his body cools, and his mind clarifies.

It's just a coincidence, he tells himself. It has to be. Still, it's just as well I've broken off contact with Spider Girl. It's up to me to restore order to this world. I have been chosen to carry out this task. Now is the time to act, he tells himself from a place of calm. I must take the right actions to protect the people I am responsible for leading. Don Wand starts his truck and drives home. When he arrives, he walks right past his mother, ignoring her request for tea, and locks himself in his room. He places his briefcase, unopened, beside the bed. He starts up his computer and bends down to pull out the box with the bottle of jawbones. He takes the disc out of its case, puts it into his hard drive, opens up the video file and converts it to an mp4. Don Wand, treasurer for the Everlasting Church of the Evangelical, logs into his unofficial e-mail account, the one with the user name, Nimrod, calls up all the addresses in his address book, most of them tithe-paying members of the church, attaches the video file, and presses send.

He shuts down the computer, and makes space at his desk for his work. He gets his rubber gloves, puts them on, takes several paper towels from the box beside the jar, and folds these to make a thick bed upon which to lay the little jawbones. He removes them from the peroxide solution with a pair of tweezers and, even though the incisors remain yellowed, he is pleased with the result, and cleans up as they dry.

Don reaches under his bed for the satin-lined box, and when he opens it up, his eyes glisten. He places the new jawbones in the box, wipes away a tear forming in the corner of one eye, and replaces the box under the bed. Don Wand, teacher, church leader, sole child and caregiver to an aging and sometimes overbearing parent, lifts his head, stands up, and goes out to make his mother a cup of tea.

THE SHADOW DANCER

STANLEY PIKE LOCKS UP THE STORM DOOR of his law office, pulls his black ball cap close over his head, slips his keys into the pocket of his burgundy leather coat ordered from Sears Catalogue, and heads for home. Into the brisk autumn evening he saunters, heading to the road that crests the town like the spine of some prehistoric giant, where his renovated two-story saltbox sits in sober attendance. From his property, Stanley can see down the house-littered valley below to the lake, and to the clear-cut scarred hills beyond. Behind his house, the land dips for a half-kilometre or so before rising sharply to the line of trees obscuring the power company's winding canal, flowing from the waters of the grand lake far in the tangled interior.

He hesitates for a moment before turning the key in the lock. He closes his eyes, smiling, and visualizes the scene that awaits him beyond the heavy metal door. Joey Small, his aging Labrador retriever, will uproot himself from the couch and stagger toward his master, tail wagging, eyes laughing, tongue cascading out over rather impressive teeth. His estranged wife, notably, will not greet him. This fact, Stanley admits without a trace of guilt, is largely the reason for his joy.

In the three months since she left him for the deputy mayor and local gas station owner, Bud Jessup, Stanley has moved through various stages of reaction: shock at how his sedentary life has been shaken up; fury that she has treated him with a distain he hardly deserved; embarrassment that he has only cottoned onto what every one else in town has apparently been aware of for months; and finally, a great pervading sense of relief that he is finally free of her judgments and recriminations. He has always known that he wouldn't be capable of keeping her interest. She'd liked his job, the quiet respect his position demanded. She'd especially liked the good steady income his work provided her, had enjoyed lording it over her friends and acquaintances. But Stanley is now able to admit, without any feeling about the matter one way or another, that she'd never liked him.

He opens the door, steps inside, and waits for Joey to make his ambling way over to greet him. Stanley bends low, taking off his cap, and offers his face to be licked. He removes his shoes and happily flings his coat across the arm of the overstuffed sofa, then proceeds into the kitchen where he grabs a diet Pepsi out of the fridge. He holds the door open (hears his wife's voice telling him how he shouldn't just stand there staring in and he imagines, with some pleasure, that she's now saying the same thing to Bud), and ponders what to eat for supper. He selects a bottle of tomato pasta sauce and some bacon, and pulls down a box of penne from the cupboard. He fries up the bacon, loving the smell. I don't care if it's bad for me, I love the damn stuff! he yells at the specter of his wife, then adds the sauce and lets it bubble while the pasta cooks. He sits to eat, every now and then offering a piece of bacon to Joey Small, who sits in attendance on him like a silent courtier and, as Stanley sips his soda, he imagines what possibilities the evening might hold.

The daylight hours are now beginning to wane as autumn releases its scent. Decaying leaves from poplar, birch, quaking aspen, and alder mingle on the earth with the thick carpet of spruce cones and larch needles now turning from green to fiery orange to reddish brown. Stanley dons his ball cap and his walking coat and shoes, and leashes his dog. They head out into the coming night, following the road to where a path branches out, like a shriveled limb, toward the canal. Other than inside his own house, this is the place where Stanley feels most at ease. Away from the penetrating eyes of neighbours, knowing their curiosity about the disintegration of his marriage, he tries not to think of their gleeful enumeration of his wife's antics, of the various attributes and shortfalls of him versus Bud. Nothing is ever said directly to him, of course, that sort of behaviour would not befit a Christian community such as this one.

Stanley releases Joey Small from his leash, knowing, after all these years together, that his stout, black friend will lope faithfully beside him because he no longer has the energy or the will to stray. They follow the path beside the canal as it traces its subtle, curving route. The only sounds are the crows bickering and the occasional squawk of a blue jay. The songbirds are deserting this lonely land for hotter, livelier places, and the fair weather walkers and the ATV crowd are staying inside to await the snow.

But for now, for this brief transitional season, the canal remains almost bereft of human activity, and it is this fortunate circumstance that allows Stanley such pleasure. He turns around and begins heading back toward town, his faithful canine close on his flank. As the sky grows darker, Stanley imagines with anticipation what he will occupy himself with for the few hours before sleep.

Stanley notices the slim outline of a figure coming toward him, and he knows, with a jolt in his gut, who this figure is. He pulls his hat low over his face; his hands upon seeing her have slicked themselves with sweat. He leans to leash Joey Small, and pulls him over to the other side of the path.

With his head bent low, his face cast away from her, Stanley strains to watch her fit, efficient body moving toward him. He tries not to look, but he can't help himself. She must be over a decade his senior, he knows, but she seems to defy the advance of age, her figure finer than that of most of the young women in town.

As they pass, Stanley averts his eyes, and resists the urge to run. He cannot look her in the face, a face he knows is as handsome as her figure.

Stanley pulls his dog close beside him and, straining to find a safe footpath on the trail to his street, makes his way home. He enters the house and removes his shoes and coat. He travels from room to room in his three-bedroom house, closing blinds and extinguishing lights. In the large living room, he draws the heavy drapes, paying special attention to sealing the seam in the middle, and leaves only one dim lamp lit. He turns on his computer and moves the beige sofa and chair back against one of the walls, so as to create an expanse of space in the centre of the room.

Joey Small hoists himself up onto the couch and settles in to watch the first half of the evening spectacle as Stanley logs onto YouTube. He chooses the fourth in a series of English Waltz lessons, and follows the instructor's directions for a short series of turns. Losing his confidence with the new steps, Stanley pauses the lesson, turns on his stereo, and plays a waltz selection on a ballroom dancing disc he ordered from eBay. He works the basic box step, finessing his posture, his sturdy arms supporting the ethereal form of the walking lady before him. When satisfied with the quality of his basic step, Stanley moves on to the underarm turn, which he performs with such grace and gallantry as to make himself flush with pleasure as well as earning a growl of approval from Joey Small. As his confidence grows, Stanley dances around the room, his greying hair darkening with moisture, as if regaining its former colour, and he employs the open arm turn in a style only slightly less than elegant. He returns to the YouTube lessons and after a couple of failed attempts, succeeds at dancing the new turns. Delighted with himself, Stanley replays the selection from the disc and waltzes his invisible lady until she begs for rest. He releases her and takes a deep, cleansing breath. He is now ready for the second half of the evening's spectacle.

There are some preparations to be made. Stanley retreats to the door under the stairs, and disappears down to the basement, reappearing a moment later with a work light attached to a stand. He sets the light up opposite the large wall of his living room, and plugs it in, Joey Small making a protest at the intensity of light by hiding his eyes with a dusty black paw. Stanley moves across the room, his body casting elongated shadows on the wall, and removes a large painting, one of a natural wetland scene he purchased at a Ducks Unlimited auction, and places it behind the sofa chair. He disappears into the basement again and returns with a camera bag and collapsed tripod. He sets the camera on the tripod at one side of the room close to and facing the large wall. He loads a new memory card and fusses with the position of the camera for a moment before hitting record.

Stanley Pike presses play on his stereo and without ceremony proceeds to remove every piece of clothing adorning his solid middle-aged body, including his socks. He steps in front of the light, the camera recording the shadow of his figure cast on the wall, and raises his arms, as if embracing a partner. He pauses for a moment, listening to the swelling waltz, and begins with the basic box step, concentrating on the smooth rising and falling of the body inherent to the dance. Losing himself in the music, Stanley begins to turn his insubstantial partner; first the basic turn, then a more complex series of double turns. Delirious now with joy at how his skill is increasing, and with his new ability to move *inside* the music, Stanley dances around the room faster and faster, his arms holding his phantom lady, a great big smile on his face.

What the camera sees is the shadow of a man's figure elongating and diminishing in relation to his proximity to the light. It captures the absence of the partner.

When the waltz ends, Stanley, his skin shiny with sweat, makes a deep bow to his fantasy friend. He takes her hand and exits the dance floor. Joey Small yawns, gets down from his front row seat and saunters through the kitchen to the door where he sits and waits for his master to let him out. Stanley quickly dresses and disassembles his film set before standing behind the door to open it just wide enough for his dog to slip out. While Joey Small takes the night air, his master busies himself with the transfer of the recording into his computer. He views it at once, and, pleased with the quality of the shadow dance, begins the process of uploading to YouTube. Stanley's pulse races with anticipation at how his third offering to the site under the pseudonym Shadow Dancing Man will be received. His first two uploads, naked shadow versions of the jive and foxtrot, were received without much interest at first, but now, to his delight, he notes the total hits at over four hundred and ninety-one thousand. Stanley opens the door to admit his dog, grinning at the idea of all those people all over the world knowing something about him that he would never share with anyone in his life. But for you, Joey Small, he says aloud.

With the upload completed, Stanley shuts down his computer for the night. He turns out the last light and retreats upstairs to his bedroom where he reads the local paper for a time before turning over and going to sleep.

After another day of settling real estate transactions and family estates, leaving the criminal cases to his younger, more ambitious partner, Stanley once again finds himself walking with his best friend in the dark beside the canal. He wears a sweater under his coat tonight, as the autumn no longer bothers to hide its cruel intentions. Stanley thinks about whether or not he is ready to begin studying the very challenging Argentine Tango and he absentmindedly whistles a tune. As he trots back toward town, his reverie is interrupted by the raucous cawing of a large murder of crows. He stops for a moment, his dog pausing beside him, and looks up into the sky where the black-winged creatures reel and pitch at one particular fellow. Something is amiss; he's ticked the rest of them off, thinks Stanley; he's done something none of the others approve of and now they'll pick and tear at him until he falls out of the sky. That's just the way of creatures, thinks Stanley as he watches, perfectly at ease with the fact that no action of his could change the course of these events happening in the sky above him. And then he turns and, in a moment when he least expects, when he is so completely unprepared for an encounter, he sees her standing, head raised to the scene in the sky. He knows that she, too, is watching events unfold, knows by her posture that she believes herself to be alone.

Stanley feels his body heat rise and almost immediately breaks into a sweat. Annoyed with himself, he leashes Joey Small, who despite a momentary protest, allows Stanley to pull him to his feet, to the other side of the dirt road and into a lope. As he nears her, Stanley catches her smell, such a pleasant womanly scent, so clean and feminine. With his head tipped away from her, his cap pulled low over his face, his eyes yearn to study her figure as she moves toward him, so agile, so sleek and powerful. And then he forces his eyes away from her, admonishing himself for looking at another man's wife in such a way, and he yanks on Joey Smalls' chain and moves past her as quickly as his legs can carry him. As he passes her by, Stanley hears her say something that sounds remarkably like the f-word. Stanley hesitates for a split second wanting to turn around, wanting to know if he really heard her say it, but he doesn't. Stanley tells himself that he'd imagined something that never really happened.

As he goes about performing his evening ritual, he decides he is not yet ready for the Argentine Tango, and opts instead to start with a simpler Latin dance, the Rumba. Stanley attempts to shake the uneasy feeling that something has occurred which remains just out of the grasp of his understanding.

Before posting to Youtube, Stanley views the shadows captured that evening. There's something different about this shadow dance. Before, his shadows seemed light, insubstantial, but these shadows dance in a restrained way somehow, as if the dancer is unable to free his shadowy soul from the confines of the earth. He seems to long for something that he cannot express. Perhaps, thinks the shadow of the dancing man, I should have been born with wings instead of feet.

ACKNOWLEDGEMENTS

A VERY VERY BIG THANK YOU TO the Newfoundland and Labrador Arts Council without whose support this book would not have existed. Many thanks to the Canada Council for the Arts as well.

Thanks to my editor, Elizabeth Phillips (whom I have never met in person), for her instructive and thorough editorial guidance. Many Thanks to Al and Jackie Forrie at Thistledown Press for taking this on.

A very heartfelt and special thank you to several of my wonderful English Literature teachers who taught me in the Catholic school system in Corner Brook, Newfoundland. To Peter Ledrew, who taught me in grade seven, and encouraged in me a love of reading, and was the first person in my life to encourage me to write. To Harold Keough, who taught me at Regina High School, and turned a blind eye when I stole copies of his novels by Dostoyevsky and Tolstoy. Thanks also to the many wonderful teachers who taught and supported me as I was growing up.

Special thanks to all of my very large family, especially my sisters Maura and Kathleen, who have been so supportive of my writing.

Special thanks to my little brother Robert, for suggesting a long time ago that I try my hand at short stories.

Special thanks to Gary Graham

Thanks also to Nick Barnes, Randall Maggs, Michelle Horacek, Janice Spencer, Mike Spencer, and Rebecca Simpson.

Inexpressible thanks to my husband, Michael Rigler, for sharing my life and work.

photo by Mike Spenser

Tara Manuel is a writer, actor, singer, puppeteer, and the Artistic Director of a production company, Shadowy Souls. She lives in Corner Brook, Newfoundland, in an old two-story house overlooking the Bay of Islands with her husband and creative partner, Michael Rigler, their two sons, Jack and Sam, and their dog Daisy. Her first book, *Filling The Belly*, was published by Thistledown Press in 2003.